Hidden Words
Hidden Worlds

CONTENTS

PREFACE

The fourteen stories that appear in this anthology are the product of a unique five-year British Council project called *Hidden Words, Hidden Worlds*.

In the early days of Myanmar's governmental transition in 2012, the British Council sought to take advantage of new freedoms in literature and travel through a programme of workshops which gave voice to previously unheard and aspiring writers from across the country. Burmese short-story writers from Yangon were trained, and then travelled to the ethnic states where, in partnership with British Council Millennium Centres and the surviving ethnic literature and culture associations, they held creative writing workshops with the public. The participants, who ranged from WW2 veterans and rubber tappers to poets and journalists, crafted and submitted stories in their own languages. Literary, linguistic and cultural leaders from each region and community were tasked with selecting the story they felt best represented their language's literature in short-story form. The stories then underwent a year of transcription, translation, editing and proofreading by more than 30 volunteers representing 11 ethnic communities.

The resulting multilingual anthology, published in Myanmar at the end of 2015, featured 28 short stories from 7 Burmese writers and 21 ethnic writers in 12 different languages. For this, the English edition, graduates of the first international literary translation workshop in Myanmar travelled to the ethnic states and worked with the writers, bridging their translation from the ethnic languages to English via Burmese, but also allowing a comparison within the two languages to ensure as true a copy as possible. As a result, this anthology will for the first time give English-speaking readers a window into the lives and literatures of Myanmar's rich, diverse and complex ethnic states.

The British Council has been established in Myanmar for more than 70 years. Our purpose is to create a friendly knowledge and understanding between the UK and countries overseas. We seek to connect people to the UK through arts and culture, through the English language and through our work in education and society. We look forward to continuing to strengthen our ties and friendship in the arts and culture sectors through programmes that give a voice to, and tell the stories of, the people of Myanmar.

Richard Sunderland
Director, British Council

INTRODUCTION

In March 1917, in Yangon, the first issue of *Thuriya* magazine published what is widely regarded as the first short story in Myanmar. Burmese literature is not so young of course, with a nearly thousand-year lineage of soldier-poetry, court dramas and religious tales to look back on; but the printing of 'Maung Thein Tin and Ma Thein Shin wuthu' by Shwe U Daung set in motion an extraordinary rise, then fall, of the Burmese short story. From the unfettered experimentation of the 1920s and 30s *Khitsan* ('Testing Times') movement to the post-colonial introspection of the 1950s and national laureate Dagon Tarya's New Literature movement, writers embraced the short story. Under the socialist military regime in the 1960s, writers became 'literary workers', tasked with upholding the national character, while works deemed unsuitable for this purpose, such as horror stories, were banned. The 1970s saw the editors of the influential *Moe Way* journal make their mark on a new generation of writers just as they confronted a deepening suppression of their craft. A brief interlude of freedom enjoyed after the 1988 revolution made way for the 1990s where the short story form had become largely ossified – though still widely popular – and constrained by the rigours of censorship. Writers continued to write, and continued to be jailed, a sword of Damocles hanging over every word until finally, in August

2012, 50 years of pre-publication censorship of the written word was formally abolished.

Although the paucity of English translations has ensured that many of the pioneers of the Myanmar short story and their modern counterparts remain unknown outside of the country – something we hope this anthology will go a small way towards addressing – the transition in Myanmar has also opened a door onto a parallel literature from the ethnic states.

The history of ethnic languages and literature from Myanmar is as complicated and diverse as the people themselves. An oft quoted, though contested, figure of 135 ethnic groups and languages is but a guess. The Mon in the south-east, along the border with Thailand, may have the oldest script in the region, dated on stone steles to at least the sixth or seventh century AD. In comparison, the numerous groups that make up the Chin, along the mountainous west and north-west border with Bangladesh and India, produced their first scripts at the end of the nineteenth century. The Kayah in the east, meanwhile, have only in the last two years been allowed to use their script, first standardised in the 1950s but then promptly outlawed.

For the last fifty years, ethnic languages and literatures have suffered under successive military governments. Teaching and writing ethnic languages and literature were, at best, discouraged and at worst criminalised in the areas under government control, unless done within the specific, narrow boundaries that the government would allow – at home, at after-school clubs, or at summer-school camps in the months of March and April. The official boundaries themselves were fluid though, changing often without notice or warning, as ethnic literatures and languages became tools in the long-running armed conflicts. In the rare periods of peace, the prospect of a freer environment to teach and write in ethnic languages would be proffered, only to be snatched away when war returned. Unsure of what was permissible, many just chose not to write at all.

In Yangon, publishers would baulk at printing a book in a script they couldn't read. Bookshops were few beyond the urban centres of Yangon and Mandalay, as were printing presses. Censors, unable to read ethnic languages, would automatically disqualify any book that was submitted to them without a Burmese-language translation, a requirement that doubled the production costs of any ethnic-language book. True, non-fiction works in ethnic languages *did* exist, mostly dissections of cultural life and rites. Crucially however, a creative tradition rooted in oral narratives had yet to make the transition to print – until now.

This anthology showcases 14 writers, including those from the Mon, Karen, Kayah, Shan, Kachin, Chin and Rakhine ethnic communities. They wrote their stories in their respective languages – Mon, Sgaw Karen, Kayah Li, Shan Gyi, Jinghpaw, Lai Hakha and Rakhine – each, with the exception of Rakhine, with their own distinct script. Unusually for an anthology, there is no central theme to anchor the stories. For these, the first short stories published in these ethnic languages, the writers were given the freedom to create and experiment without being constrained by externally imposed thematic or stylistic rules. If a theme does emerge from the collection, it would be one of place and time. The stories range from the urban Yangon street (Yu Ya's 'Silenced Night') to the rural Kayah village (Maw Ma Thae's 'Love of Ka Nya Maw'); from the colonial era (Saw Lambert's 'Kaw Tha Wa the Hunter') through the 1960s military regime (Lay Ko Tin's 'The Moon That Shone Within') to the peace treaties in Mon State of the early 1990s (Min Yar Moe's 'The Right Answer'), and into modern-day Kachin State (Mali Hku Shini's 'A Bridge Made from Cord').

For ease of reading, and where possible, they have been organised geographically, according to the dominant location of the story, and not necessarily grouped by ethnic identity of the writer or the language in which the story was first created. Each story is accompanied by a brief remark to set the scene and headed by a title written in the original script.

It is doubtful whether many of these stories would have passed the feared censor-board had they been published only a few years ago. Min Yar Moe's description of using government newspapers to roll cheroots would certainly have felt the censors' ire, as would Myint Win Hlaing's depiction of a pregnancy outside marriage. The Abbot and Saya in Ah Phyu Yaung (shwe)'s story of power and corruption would never have been allowed to strike up a friendship, while Letyar Tun's 'The Court Martial' would almost certainly have resulted in a trial of his own. The fact that these stories were printed in Myanmar without restriction demonstrates the difference in climate in just a few short years – though the shadow of censorship hasn't yet diminished.

I remember one morning sitting in a teashop in Botahtaung Township, Yangon. At my table were half a dozen writers, two of whom feature in this book – Sayar Lay Ko Tin and Letyar Tun. They had first been imprisoned in the 1960s and 1980s respectively. To our right, a smaller, more sombre table was occupied by four men, writers too, who met there once a week to remember those with whom they were imprisoned in the 1970s. Farther back, a larger group of journalists, noisier and more boisterous than others, were celebrating the recent release of two of their colleagues from jail in Mon State. Five decades of imprisoned writers in a single teashop. This is not unusual in Yangon.

A century after the publication of that first short story from Myanmar, it is my hope, then, that soon writers of *all* languages in Myanmar will sit in teashops and celebrate not just surviving, but the publication of yet another book of their stories to be read and enjoyed around the world.

A NOTE ON NAMES AND TERMS:

For the purposes of this anthology, 'Myanmar' refers to the nation, 'Burmese' to the people, language and literature. References to the ethnic groups and languages, where possible, have retained the English transliteration preferred by the original writer, so 'Karen' remains 'Karen' and not 'Kayin', and 'Kayah' is used rather than the older 'Karenni'. Where the writer expressed no preference – and in the face of a multitude of possible transliterations – the most commonly found form (in this editor's opinion) has been used, such as 'Lashio' rather than 'Larshio', 'La Shio' or 'Lasio'.

A number of words and terms from the original languages of Myanmar appear in the translations that follow, and they are usually rendered in *italic* on their first appearance in a story. Definitions are given in the story and/or in the glossary on page 148.

Lucas Stewart

LAY KO TIN

Lay Ko Tin (b.1947) is an award winning poet, short story writer, novelist, translator and editor. A former political prisoner, having spent more than ten years incarcerated under two different regimes, he has published 15 books including *Last Day Scenes of Politicians* (2015) which recounts the final hours of prisoners before their execution. He is senior editor for the acclaimed Seikku Cho Cho annual short story anthology and has sat on the selection board for several of the leading independent literary awards in Myanmar including the Shwe Amyutae and Salai Tin Maung Oo awards. He is currently a member of the editorial board for *Khit Ya Nant* journal in Yangon.

THE MOON THAT SHONE WITHIN

After the military coup of 1962, many school children were imprisoned for demonstrating on the streets of Yangon. Sayar Lay Ko Tin was among them. This tender love story is thus a personal tribute to those who fought for democracy and paid for it with their youth. A young student, Soe Kyaw begins a relationship with an ethnic Mon girl. As he learns more about her, he encounters a culture simultaneously familiar and strange, lessons in love cruelly cut off after his arrest by Military Intelligence. 'The Moon That Shone Within' is notable, not as a glorified account of the horrors of incarceration for these children – a trap Sayar Lay Ko Tin avoids – but as a longing for the lives outside the walls that continue on without them.

THE MOON THAT SHONE WITHIN

ရင်ထဲမှာ သာသော လ

My last trip was on a large ocean-going ship to Myeik, the southernmost city in Myanmar. I've never been to Mawlamyine, the capital of Mon State, and have been just once to the Kyaikhtiyo Pagoda, one of the most renowned pagodas in Myanmar, but only after I reached quite a great age.

Travelling provides me with an excuse to improve my knowledge of the diverse places and people in my country. Before I go somewhere I always do my research. I study the history and people, famous sites and incidents. While on the road, I jot down notes in my diary every day. Inevitably, I began to write articles, essays and short stories about my travels.

Travelogues have long been popular in Myanmar. I've always enjoyed reading them: Theikpan Maung Wa, Zawgyi and Min Thu Wun's accounts of their journeys to England; Dagon Thaya's *The Traveller, The Ayeyarwaddy* and *The Yangtze and the Volga*; Mya Than Thint's award-winning *Record of a Trip to Pondaung-Ponnya*; Ludu U Hla's well-known *Trip to Japan*, as well as his wife Ludu Daw Ama's *Inland People Must Travel to the Sea*.

Unexpected things can happen at any time and often revive old memories. The smell of fruit in the market, or music from a teashop radio often remind me of someone from the past, especially of my early memories of a Mon girl I loved, the mangosteens she offered me and the sound of the Mon *Thingyan* festival.

When I was young, I lived with my parents in South Oakkala Township, Yangon. As a ninth standard student, I had a few close friends who lived nearby and we'd play football or *chinlon* together. Sometimes, we'd go to a teashop and play chess or take a bus to the snooker hall. Most of my friends were the same age as me, though a few were like our older brothers. One of them in particular would take us younger brothers to the Shwedagon Pagoda to enjoy the *Thabaung* Festival and the Thingyan water festival.

His name was Ko Thet Lwin. He was a middle-aged bachelor, although there were a lot of women who were in love with him. He was the only son of a widow and he lived with his mother in a two-storey house in a large compound, where we would sometimes eat and stay the night. One time, he made friends with a young woman and her teenage sister from Mon State who had come to visit a mutual friend. He took them to see the pagodas, Kandawgyi Lake and Bogyoke Market, and beginning with the next time they came to Yangon, they stayed at his house. One time, they came with the third member of their family, the youngest sister, a beautiful student the same age as me.

One day, Ko Thet Lwin invited me to visit the Shwedagon Pagoda with the spinster Mi Yin San and her two teenage sisters Mi Yin Hla and Mi Hla Chote. We paid homage to the Golden Pagoda, Ko Thet Lwin and Mi Yin San in front, the two sisters and I behind them kneeling on our shins. Mi Hla Chote handed me some offering flowers. She bowed once and looked up to the blue sky, closed her eyes, with hands raised palm-to-palm to her forehead in obeisance, then bowed thrice to the pagoda. I didn't bow because I was holding the flowers, but when she finished paying homage, she reached out to take the bundle of flowers with a nod and a smile. A bright smile lit up her fair, sweet face, her wide, round eyes shining through dark eyelashes.

I then also bowed three times and we all walked a full circle around the pagoda in a clockwise direction. Talking to each other, Ko Thet Lwin and Mi Yin San walked in front. The two sisters and I followed. Mi Hla Chote spoke once in a while, but Mi Yin Hla looked here and there and didn't speak at all. Not until she blurted out with a strong Mon accent, "I'd like to pay homage to the Shin Sawbu Buddha image."

At Shwedagon, there is a *su htaung pyi* ('wish fulfilling') Buddha image donated by Mon Queen Shin Sawbu. One of the nine wonders of the Golden Pagoda, it is well known among not just Mon and Burmese people, but all the ethnic groups of the country. The Mon queen was the only woman who was crowned queen by four consecutive kings. She never forgot her duty in giving donations to build pagodas, construct monasteries and sponsor men to become monks in the Buddhist order. The queen passed away in Dagon – present-day Yangon – at the age of 79 in the Myanmar year 834 (1471). One more fact I learned about Shin Sawbu: her crown is in the Victoria and Albert Museum in London. To be honest, I actually knew little about the Mon queen before that day, but Mi Hla Chote told me all about her.

Mi Hla Chote and I grew closer after visiting Shwedagon. The next day, we all went to Kandawgyi Lake and the zoological garden. While we talked, Mi Yin Hla interrupted every now and then in Mon language.

"What did she say?" I asked Mi Hla Chote.

"She told me to invite you to Mawlamyine."

The three sisters went back to Mawlamyine a few days later. Ko Thet Lwin, myself and some friends saw them off at the Yangon railway station, waving goodbye as the train pulled away.

* * *

I had planned to visit Mawlamyine with friends during the December school holidays, but Mi Yin San and her two sisters suddenly showed up in Yangon, so we cancelled our trip. The three sisters stayed at Ko Thet Lwin's house as usual. They went to visit Kyaik Kauk Pagoda in Thanlyin and Ye Le Pagoda on a river islet nearby. I, of course, went with them, so I had breakfast that day and dinner the next at Ko Thet Lwin's house. One night, while the two younger sisters and I were talking after dinner, Ko Thet Lwin and Mi Yin San went out leaving the three of us behind.

"Brother, let's have some mangosteens," said Mi Hla Chote,

getting up from her seat and returning with a bowl. She peeled a mangosteen and gave it to me. I hesitated to take it as I was a bit embarrassed to accept a piece of fruit peeled by a girl I was falling for.

"She made the offer in the spirit of good will, enjoy it," said Mi Yin Hla.

"Yes, if that is what she wants," I said, unable to hide my happiness.

"We'll bring some durians next time. Do you like durian?" Mi Yin Hla asked me.

"Yes, very much," I replied, mimicking Mi Yin Hla's Mawlamyine accent, which made Mi Hla Chote smile. Her smile was simple and innocent and contagious. We talked in turns, about our parents, our schools and the towns we lived in. Eventually, Ko Thet Lwin and Mi Yin San returned. It was getting late, so I made my excuses.

As I left, I noticed Mi Hla Chote was the only one who waved goodbye. Mi Yin San and her sisters soon went back to Mawlamyine, taking with them things they could sell at their stall in the local market. Once again I went with friends to see them off at the railway station. Before the train left, I had a chance to speak to Mi Hla Chote one last time, she leaning out of the window, I standing on the platform.

"Final exams are coming up. Work hard at your studies, Soe Kyaw," said Mi Hla Chote.

"I'm sure to pass. I've never failed an exam, Mi," I replied confidently.

"We'll see," she said in her strong Mawlamyine accent, and I just couldn't help smiling.

She asked me to write, so I wrote my first-ever love letter to her. She replied immediately, reminding me to work hard to pass my exams. She and her sisters would come to Yangon as soon as they had spare time, but they'd also like to invite me and my friends to their village in Mon State for the Thingyan Festival in April. That was all she wrote. No expression of love that I'd hoped for, but it gave me something to look forward to. A few weeks later I took the exam and, as usual, I did well.

* * *

April came, and with it the sisters to Yangon. Just before Thingyan, many *pandal* stages had been constructed around the city, some for people to throw water on the crowds below, others for dancing and *thangyat* competitions. Thangyat chants are an old tradition, in which people are free to satirise difficulties and unjust treatment under their rulers. Naturally the military regime discouraged such chanting, so kids my age didn't know much about it.

As per Mi Hla Chote's invitation, Ko Thet Lwin, myself and a friend named Tun Yee went back with them to Mawlamyine. The Thingyan Festival in Mawlamyine is famous as the best water festival in the country, but we didn't go to Mawlamyine. Instead we celebrated Thingyan in their hometown Mudon, about 15 miles south of the city. Their Thingyan festival was very traditional, very Mon. On the eve of Thingyan, men hauled massive piles of sand on oxcarts to the local monastery where they held a sand pagoda-building contest on the last day of the festival. The next day, a big crowd came to enjoy the singing and dancing. Food stalls popped up everywhere, offering free Mon curry and rice to all the festival-goers.

With Mi Yin San in the lead, we wandered around eating the Mon Thingyan rice called *pein thaik*. It gave off a waxy smell and there was water in it – very strange for us from Yangon – but eaten together with dried fish, fried fish paste, mangoes, garlic and chili peppers, it was delicious. Everywhere we walked in town, people threw water on us. Although we'd already eaten Thingyan rice at one house, we couldn't refuse to eat again at the next. Ko Thet Lwin was a big eater, but Tun Yee and I couldn't stomach much. Mi Hla Chote seemed particularly pleased to watch us eating.

Myanmar's New Year comes right after Thingyan and the sand-pagoda building festival started in the village monastery. The presiding monk preached the Five Precepts of Buddhism. Everyone old and young, men and women, worked together to pile up sand and fashion the basic shape of the pagoda. Ko Thet Lwin and I helped carry buckets of sand. When we paused to take a rest, Mi Yin San brought us cold drinks. Mi Yin Hla and her boyfriend threw water at each other, then they came over and splashed us as well, followed by Mi Hla Chote who only poured water on me.

"Here, throw some back at her," said Mi Yin Hla, handing me a bowl of water. Mi Hla Chote stood still with her back towards me, her two pigtails hanging loosely in front. I didn't mean to pour the whole bowl of water on her dress, which was already sopping wet, but when I stammered an embarrassed apology she just gave me a dazzling smile. "I'll send you a letter in Yangon, Soe Kyaw," Mi Hla Chote told me later.

Back in Yangon, a pink envelope soon arrived containing a letter with only two words in Mon. I didn't know one word of Mon, so I had to ask Ko Thet Lwin for help. He smiled gently when he read the letter. "I've known about you two for a long time."

"You think big sister San knows too?" I asked.

"She already knows. They'll come on the full-moon day in the month of *Kason*."

I didn't know what to say. The only thing I knew was that Ko Thet Lwin and Mi Yin San would get engaged either in the month of Thadingyut or Thasaungmon. But what future lay in store for me and Mi Hla Chote?

I replied to her letter immediately with a poem relating the first-ever heartaches of a boy for a girl counting the days until he can be with her again. I had caught the heart of the one I adored, the one I'd always seen off at the railway station, the one I built pagodas with. It was the happiest, most unforgettable day of my life.

* * *

Although I had friends in my neighbourhood, I hardly had any at school. The few friends I did have were fond of reading. Not only school textbooks, but also novels, non-fiction and especially books on politics. I often borrowed books from them. A voracious reader, I often forgot to eat or sleep, but I never forgot to write to Mi Hla Chote. The two of us in my letters were like the main characters of a romance story. Her words were like poetry, and she often filled her envelopes with beautiful flower petals. I missed her especially on full-moon nights, leaving my bedroom windows open since she'd written in one of her letters, "Soe, look at the moon because I too am watching. Although we're far away, it's if we are together."

One day when I returned from school, Hla Htay, a close friend of mine who lived in the same street, was taken from his house by the police on orders from the local Burma Socialist Programme Party committee. His uncle U Hla Oo had also been taken the week before. I went to Hla Htay's grandfather's house to ask what happened and was told U Hla Oo, an accountant at a state-owned Cooperative Enterprise in Shan State, had led a strike in the so-called 5 Division Protest soon after the government cancelled peace talks with armed ethnic groups. Maybe that's why Hla Htay was also taken in for questioning.

Shortly after that, my cousin's husband was also arrested at his office, and then they came for me. I didn't have the slightest clue why. I was locked up in the Military Intelligence compound and then transferred to Insein Jail. I was kept in isolation in a torture room for a while, then sent from one place to another. Twenty-four hours, forty-eight hours passed. Days became a year, two years, three years. The seasons had already turned from hot to rainy to cold three times – three whole years in a prison cell!

I'd been told, "We'll meet together at the full moon, Soe." I missed you, Mi Hla Chote. I was locked up all day and allowed out only ten minutes to shower. My nights were spent in solitary confinement with a dim lightbulb. What was day and what was night? They'd stolen my nights, I could hardly remember the shimmering moon. Where was the moon? "Mi, I can still see you, even though there's no moon."

With the end of parliamentary democracy and the beginning of authoritarian rule, the country fell into utter chaos. The BSPP was the only party. Politicians from different organisations, students union activists, writers, poets, journalists and editors were arrested under irreversible orders from the authorities. I was only one of many.

As young students, many of us had girlfriends and we suffered being separated from them. We longed for the letters from our loved ones. Those who had wives and children were allowed to receive letters from them once every two or three months. We students also received letters once in a while from our families, but never from our girlfriends. Our future was vague, neither black nor white. Every now and then we might get scraps of newspaper with announcements of engagements or weddings. We didn't dare to look. Instead, we'd ask someone else, with a tremor in our voices, to read the names listed.

The saying 'time is the best medicine' was not true for us. We younger inmates tended to remember those outside for a very long time. And to make things worse, we were classified as political prisoners, which meant we were repeatedly sent from jail to jail for questioning. Maybe the heaviest burden of all was to stay true to our belief that the new regime was false.

* * *

It was a long journey for us young students. Along the way we got to meet many renowned writers, poets and journalists from whom our knowledge of literature grew. When finally we were allowed books, we read them cover to cover. Many of us learned English from those writers.

Many years passed. Four or five for some, nine or ten for others; a number were given life sentences on a prison island in the middle of the ocean. I myself was released after some four years. I didn't continue my studies. I stayed with my family and started to work for a living, yet, thanks to my prison routine, I kept up my reading. Then inspiration just came. I started to write and translate stories. Finally, a job I loved. I sent my work to magazines and when some pieces were selected, I was extremely happy to see my writing in print and published.

I was not happy in every way, though. The question of Mi Hla Chote overtaxed my heart. I asked my friends, but heard only vague reports of Ko Thet Lwin and Mi Yin San, far less about the two younger sisters.

"Ko Thet Lwin and Mi Yin San are in Mawlamyine. They got married."

"Can it be true?" I wondered. I stood in stunned silence, a statue. My heart drooped, refusing to believe it, until one day Tun Yee spelled it all out in detail.

I still remember she once told me, "We'll meet face-to-face at the full moon, Soe."

Ah! I've known moonless nights in jail, years of moonless nights. So many I can't count them all. Yet even now that I'm out, I've lost the moon that shone within me. Lost forever, I know, never to be regained. A long journey encounters uncertain roads, so all I can do is think of it as an ugly misfortune that could happen to anyone.

"Just let it be, Mi."

Translated from Burmese to English by Dr Mirror (Taunggyi)

MIN YAR MOE

Min Yar Moe (b.1977) is an ethnic Mon writer and
rubber trader from Thoung Pha Lu village in
Mon State. His articles and poems, published in
underground Mon language journals, explore
the dynamics between national politics and the
Mon people, often depicting Western and Asian
intellectuals and thinkers. He currently lives in a Mon-
speaking village in Karen State where he stood in the
2015 general election for the Mon National Party. He
writes under the pen name Ahpor Rahmonya.

THE RIGHT ANSWER

Given the current political climate in Myanmar, it is
inevitable a story centred on the conflicts would
emerge, though here Min Yar Moe has crafted a
scene of peace rather than war, where his narration is
inspired by an actual series of ceremonies held across
Mon State to mark the historic peace treaty between
the central government and the rebel New Mon State
Party in 1994. Originally writing in the Mon language,
Min Yar Moe reports on the opulent ceremony as an
eye witness with rigorous detail, before unmasking
the state lies and propaganda through the personal
voice of the headmistress Mi Shin Thant. Set over a
single afternoon, the events of 'The Right Answer' are
fifty years in making, and yet, through understated
imagery, Min Yar Moe leaves the reader in no doubt
that the true consequences of that afternoon
have yet to be seen.

THE RIGHT
ANSWER

သွဟ်ခုၚ်

No one knows what to call the flowers. There seems to be no word for them in Mon. Small leaves, perennial, green and tough, fearing neither rain nor sun, the red clusters bloom like little fists. Every house in town grows them, trimmed nice and pretty. At my aunt and uncle's house they run along the border with their neighbour's property, so striking that passers-by often ask, "What's that flower?"

And what do they say? "No idea. It's a hedge flower."

Ninety-nine out of a hundred people would answer the same. A hedge flower! Of course, everybody knows the Burmese name; a century hence people will still call it *ponneyeik*. Or in English, 'wild geranium' or even 'jungle flame'. But if you told them the real name, the Mon name, they wouldn't have a clue what you were talking about. Just another word from our language that has disappeared. And the sad thing is, people don't even know it's been forgotten. It reminds me of what my aunt used to say when I was little: 'Don't knot your *longyi* too high or your bottom will show." Embarrassing if it does, but even more shameful if you didn't know it could, such is the way of the world.

* * *

It was New Year's Eve 1995. The flowers in front of the Sermon Hall were in full bloom, here a single flower, there a bunch, braving the summer heat to creep around the building, though they'd been pruned back numerous times.

The monastery compound was crowded. An unusual number of venerable abbots and monks milled about; people filled the rest house and crouched underneath the large acacia trees in the courtyard. Literature and Culture Committee members, the Mon Dhamma group, aldermen and townsfolk and everyone from the outlying villages had put aside their fears and come. Visibly excited, they knew it was a special day and whispered to their friends, "What a turnout!"

Mi Shin Thant, Headmistress of Than Hpyu Zayat Town No. 1 Basic Education High School, had been personally invited. Even she, a veteran of many public gatherings and talks, felt a chill run down her spine. But unlike the others, it wasn't due to excitement. The large crowd, the unusual number of monks – it all unsettled her.

She'd grown up in the age of fear. She remembered when a neighbour, a kind man, had harvested that quarter's rice yield. It wasn't much, barely enough to feed his family. Yet he failed to give his quota to the local authorities, so they came and took what rice they could find in his barn. A rubber tapper, living in the far end of her village, was also arrested for not presenting his due to the township officer. Someone's father went to the rice mill in Than Hpyu Zayat saying he'd return with sticky rice sweets and bananas for the village, but was abducted along with his oxcart. They never did find out if he was dead or alive. Not that it mattered, either way he'd end up in the same place: if he was dead, he'd be buried in a hole for the rest of his days; if alive, he'd sleep in one the rest of his nights.

The worst thing about growing up in an age of fear was living like a ghost. Come dusk, they'd wash quickly at the tank in back of the house, eat dinner before night fell, put out the lights, and sneak out to the hole. Long and shallow with bamboo mats crammed inside, it was their sleeping pit. There, she and her family would lie still, listening as the whole village went silent except for the inauspicious caw of a bird. And then dogs barking. Their hearts would fill with apprehension, nobody dared breathe. Oh Buddha, *Dhamma, Sangha*! Was it robbers, soldiers, secret police? After the barking came the *bong, bong, bong* of the signal gong. It was a gang of robbers. They'd hear the bad news – which house was broken into, what was taken, who was taken – but they were safe in the sleeping pit.

Daytime was no easier. On Sabbath days when discussions of religion and community, the attainment of nirvana or construction works for the temple strayed into talk of the government, the Abbot would warn everyone: "Stop, stop! The walls have ears." Then no one dared utter another word.

No wonder Mi Shin Thant couldn't shake off the feeling something was about to happen.

* * *

The monastery courtyard was more packed than a pagoda festival. Even Headmistress Mi Shin Thant couldn't suppress her surprise, and whispered to the man next to her: "I've never seen such as crowd before, not even in the city."

Despite the crowd, ten men stood out. Their white, cotton shirts tucked into a bright red and white checked *longyi* caused everyone there to stare and murmur, "How brave they are, nobody wears Mon garb in public." The ten men filed between the people and along the perimeter of the courtyard, and as the appointed time approached, they assembled next to the main stage to see that everything was in readiness. They tested the knots holding up the giant red banner emblazoned in white letters *Government and New Mon State Party Ceasefire Ceremony*. They took one last look at the golden *hongsa* bird symbols on the stage, placed as if ready to fly away with the essence of what it means to be Mon. The men double-checked the position of the two lecterns centre stage and cast an eye on the six rows of chairs now occupied by monks and notables from the town. Only the front row was empty, as everyone waited for the VIPs to arrive.

At 12:30 sharp, a fancy car drove up and five men in their 30s got out. The front passenger was dressed in his finest Mon colours; the others wore plain *longyi* and white shirts. Four of the ceremony volunteers came to greet the front passenger. As they made their way up the central aisle to the foot of the stage, all eyes fixed on the strangers. One man standing beside Mi Shin Thant poked his friend and jutted his head towards the men to ask, "Are they from Military Intelligence?"

"No way. MI faces never look that calm."

"Then who are they? Reporters?"

His friend shrugged. He didn't know. Nobody in the audience did.

At 12:45, ten of the ceremony volunteers burst into action, rushing around the courtyard, giving signals to each other and glancing at the five men by the stage. One of the strangers pulled out a walkie-talkie, held it to his ear and repeated a message to his four colleagues who turned to face the sound of approaching vehicles.

Into the compound drove five cars, even more expensive than the first, guarded front and behind by two large trucks. The convoy stopped, thirty soldiers jumped out of the trucks and took up positions around the courtyard and throughout the monastery compound. Eleven men, proud in traditional Mon garb, stepped out of the car. A man of composure and dignity, aged about seventy-five, led the group towards the Sermon Hall, where the ceremony would take place. They paid their respects to the crowd, of both monks and farmers, before taking their seats in the vacant front row. The sight of these men, heroes forced to live in the jungle far from the towns, bowing to everyone regardless of profession or social standing, awed the crowd. These were the VIPs everyone had been waiting for, the leaders of the New Mon State Party.

The Abbot of Myo Taw Oo monastery school proclaimed to the audience: "May today's historical occasion be as successful as King Dhammaceti's fostering of the Buddhist *sasana*."

At that, a hush fell over the crowd.

* * *

Outside the Sermon Hall, latecomers stood in the afternoon sun. There was no more room inside to witness the ceremony, but they didn't care. It gave them a chance to study the Mon soldiers. Many of the townsfolk had never seen a Mon soldier before, yet they all agreed: "They look more decent than Burmese soldiers."

They were also looking for reporters. They expected an event such as this would appear on the state-run MRTV eight o'clock news, as well as in government newspapers like *The New Light of Myanmar* and *Mirror*. Everyone knew the media well. They often used the papers to roll their cheroots.

An old man, sitting away from the rest under a shade tree, gritted his teeth. He'd once been a Mon soldier and, gazing on their leopard-camouflage uniforms, memories of his struggle for the Mon cause came flooding back. "Ah, to be young again like them!" he sighed.

* * *

At 1:00, the emcee hailed the historic importance of the day's events. A bilateral ceasefire agreement had been made between the Myanmar government and the New Mon State Party, ceremonies having already been held in the Mon cities Moulmein and Mudon. He read out the day's agenda, one item after another, and even simple farmers in the crowd, far more concerned with harvests than politics, listened intently to the leaders.

Chairman Naing Shwe Kyin of the New Mon State Party was the first to speak. No one had expected him to be so eloquent. Up next was Naing Tin Aung, who explained, "We agreed to this ceasefire because the Party believes this is the only way to save the lives of our Mon people. If we're mistaken, if this decision proves wrong, then we take full responsibility for our actions and will accept your judgement, however history may record us."

At this, the crowd broke into applause. Whispers spread that he was a local man, the son of Naing Aung Tun from Pa Nga village, and the applause grew louder.

The last speaker of the day announced by the emcee was a general. As he took the stage, everyone stared with interest, especially when he explained about the Mon Army. The villagers might not follow politics but everyone knew the word 'war', and here was a real Mon soldier, a Mon warrior. He spoke in Burmese, so all would be able to understand him.

Unlike the previous speakers, the general was not interrupted with applause. The crowd was silent with their own thoughts, attempting to reconcile the false image they had read of Mon soldiers with the composed and proud man standing in front of them. The villagers had always been told that the Mon insurgents, the rebels, the traitors, looked like beasts with long hair and shaggy beards.

Headmistress Mi Shin Thant was quiet for another reason. Ever since the general appeared on the stage she couldn't shake the feeling that he looked familiar. The emcee had addressed him as general Htaw Mon, a name she had heard somewhere before. But where could she have met a Mon soldier, least of all a general? Only when the general had finished, bringing the ceremony to a close, did it suddenly come to her who he was. Of course she'd heard that name before, though he hadn't been a general then, just plain Htaw Mon, an old friend from her school days. So that's who these Mon soldiers are, she thought, not rebels and insurgents, just classmates and neighbours.

* * *

The convoy drove away and the crowd dispersed, following the trail of flowers blooming along the monastery wall like always. No one needed to know the flowers' true name to appreciate their beauty. It made no more difference than playing a harp to a buffalo. Likewise, all the often heard but seldom understood words – *Mon Front Army, New Mon State Party, Mon National Liberation Army, truce, ceasefire* – meant little to the people of Than Hpyu Zayat that afternoon. What did matter were the people behind the words. The Mon community, realising how they'd been deceived in the past, had seen the truth standing before them.

Translated from Mon to Burmese anonymously,
and from Burmese to English by San Lin Tun

MI CHAN WAI

Mi Chan Wai (b.1953) is an award winning writer and teacher, born in Tha Htone, Mon State. She has published more than 21 books including novels, short stories, and travel articles exploring the lives of fishermen and pearl divers in the Myeik Archipelago. One of these, a novella, *Anesthetic*, on the empowerment of women in crayfish farming, was translated into Japanese and included in a publication by the Toyota Foundation of Japan in 2003. Her last collection, *Heart Broken Oyster and other Sea Stories,* won a National Literature Award in 2000.

READING THE HEART OF THE SEA

The relationship between the diverse ethnic groups in Myanmar is bound by multifaceted elements which remain a significant – if not paramount – concern to this day. In 'Reading the Heart of the Sea', originally published in *Kalyar* Magazine, Mi Chan Wai explores this relationship through the more innocent eyes of youth. Here, the narrative – alternating between first and third person - draws on the seascape world of the Hsalon people in the far south of Myanmar, where a celebration of Hsalon cultural identity augments the sense of 'otherness' from those on the mainland. For the dual protagonists, Oh Oh and Cherry, this 'otherness' which attracts those seeking the exotic on Bocho island, is absent; instead, a brief encounter leads to a longer lasting attraction.

READING THE HEART OF THE SEA

ပင်လယ်ရဲ့ အတွင်းသားကိုဖွင့်ဖတ်

Oh Oh was very happy today. Looking east toward the coast of Lampi Island like always, who'd ever seen so many motorboats docking at the village? Oh Oh stayed to watch the last of the timber and bamboo get unloaded and only then remembered to go home. Father was busy dealing with strangers, but seemed to know why Oh Oh was late. "Oh Oh Boy," he called out, "Father and everyone's going to celebrate the Bocho Island Hsalon Festival. You'll should come help."

"A Hsalon Festival?" Oh Oh didn't understand. Oh Oh was half-Hsalon and knew what Hsalon meant. Oh Oh's mother was Hsalon, a native of the sea, but Father was born to the far north in Pakokku. So how did an inlander from upper Myanmar come to these shores and fall in love with a Hsalon? Father had found work in Myeik, then came to Bocho Island via Bokepyin to buy sea products from Hsalon divers who gathered sea cucumbers, wing oysters, ambergris and sea cradle. He'd sell their catch to folks who could afford to eat and drink as they please. Father's Hsalon traders were in and out of the house all the time.

It was strange to hear Father talk about a festival in the village. What kind of festival? Some kind of performance? Ask Father and I was sure to be scolded. And Mother would only tell me whatever Father said was true. Father made the decisions at home.

The villagers heeded Father's words. If anything happened,

they'd come and consult him. Father was the main uplander among them. Neither Oh Oh nor the others had seen many uplanders except for the soldiers who sometimes came to the island.

Pressing his hands against his head, Father once told Oh Oh, "A man's got to have a good head on his shoulders." Oh Oh was already a fourth grader, old enough to understood he meant a good brain. "Oh Oh Boy, Son, you need your schooling. Your Mother gave birth to you, so for sure you're ethnic Hsalon. But Hsalon or not, you need an education. If you're uneducated, you'll be trampled down. When seafaring Hsalons fall into debt, they never see the end of it. They're too illiterate to read others' fine print."

Father often said things like that. When we both went out to the western shore just as the sun was setting, Father spelled it out patiently. "Son, soon you'll be grown. You should know your people. Hsalons depend on the sea for their livelihood, but many more die than are born. The government helps to remedy the problem with villages and schools, and now they've organised this festival to raise the profile of the Hsalons. Visitors will come from town, so we locals have to build guesthouses and clinics for them. There's not enough room on this slope for building guesthouses, so now I'm trying to find more space on the far side of the hill. Do what you can to help, my son. By the way, what about that collection of yours? If you have any beautiful shells, give them to me – or rather, lend them. I want to display rare items at my Hsalon produce kiosk."

"Yes, Father. I got some shells from the fishing boats. All kinds of sea life. Oh Oh doesn't know what they're called in Burmese. Will any theatre groups come and perform?"

"You bet. Also dancers from Dawei and Kawthaung, and our local Hsalon dancers."

"Gosh, sounds wonderful!"

Father smiled and looked on as Oh Oh ran up the sandy beach overjoyed in anticipation. Oh Oh couldn't wait to tell the good news to friends at school.

* * *

School, however, closed from the next day to let the teachers help with festival preparations, which made the students happy. Boards and bamboo poles were piled up high in front of the house. The locals chatted non-stop, carefree children tumbled happily on the beach. Oh Oh followed Father, pretending to keep busy. People recognised Father's son and greeted me "Oh Oh" here and "Oh Oh" there. How popular I was!

As the festival drew closer, Mother wore herself out cleaning because guests from town would stay at their house. Father said, "Oh Oh Boy, help your mother. VIPs will come and stay with us". What were these VIPs? Oh Oh later learned Father meant "very important persons". Let them come. The whole island was bustling, building kiosks and readying water supplies. Honestly, up to then there'd only been one or two wells for drinking water, but with so many people coming, everyone was digging deep wells and fitting taps. There were so many strange new things no one had ever seen before, so many guesthouses and toilets being built for the VIPs. Why did their toilets have to be different from those for everyone else?

"Foreigners who come will also use toilets like this. They're fascinated by Hsalons, how we dive for things from the seabed and live with nature." Oh Oh asked Father what living with nature was, but he just laughed. His white teeth looked nice, nothing like Hsalon men and women who chewed betel that coated their teeth with black crud. How ugly they were! Father's skin was also whiter, more handsome than Oh Oh.

"Your Mae Mae is lucky, your Mae Mae is very lucky," said Wu Kyu's *Anaung*, the Hsalon endearment for mother. Oh Oh called Mother *Mae Mae*, like people from Myeik and Bokepyin, a little different from Hsalons. Father, however, did not like Oh Oh to call him *Apaung* like the locals. Nothing unusual about that, he was Burmese after all. The weird thing was that Father never returned to upper Myanmar. Oh Oh never knew why. Father used to talk about upper Myanmar, but he never said a word about returning there. Mae Mae might want to go for a visit with him, but to live there? Hmph!

"Remember, Oh Oh, Hsalons like Mae Mae love the sea. They

never live where the Burmese do. If Mae Mae went and stayed there, your *Ahbon* would not be happy. And if Ahbon isn't happy, Mae Mae won't be happy either."

Ahbon was Oh Oh's mother's father, *Ahpo* in Burmese. Oh Oh had no *Ahpwa*, so Ahbon lived with another daughter in Don Pale'aw. When they stayed in Ahbon's village during vacation, he enjoyed learning to swim. When Ahbon came, he brought seafood treats like *thepalok* and *wapalok*. Ahbon would come to the Hsalon Festival too. There'd be lots of good times.

Tomorrow was the eve of Hsalon Festival. Boats and ships would bring visitors from Myeik and Kawthaung. Wouldn't it be great if Oh Oh's favourite movie stars Wailu Kyaw and Khaing Thin Kyi came from Yangon, too. Oh Oh also wanted to see foreigners, and maybe even to greet them, "How are you?", like the teachers at school had taught.

* * *

When the guests arrived at the island, the scene made everyone giddy. So many people! Men wearing hats, jeans and jackets. Women with red hair, yellow hair, dark glasses. Oh Oh could hardly decide whom to watch amidst such a dizzying scene.

Oh! Lu'awhi, nakyi'hsam, jalan'kattaing, oh! Kujet nakyi'hsan. An unfamiliar Hsalon song played when someone pressed a button. Oh Oh didn't like it as much as Mae Mae's group dancing at celebrations and spirit rituals in the village.

Men beat aluminum rice pots and plastic buckets. Women sang enthusiastically. Was that the same Hsalon song the press-button machine played? And the stupid clothes the dancers wore, was that supposed to be a Hsalon costume? Oh Oh could not help laughing. Real Hsalon women traditionally went bare on top. The Dawei girls balancing water pots on their heads were alluring and the group dancing to the song *Yahe'shin* was also attractive. During the intermission, Oh Oh left the audience stands and pushed through the sweaty crowd. Whew! I went to the beach for a breath of fresh air, but the place was swarming with people. So I made for the less frequented western shore where people went for a peaceful swim.

Oh Oh climbed the slope past the guesthouses, up a winding path through the woods. All alone, I suddenly heard a sound. Someone was crying, a young girl about my same age, wearing a skirt with yellow flowers.

"Young girl, young visitor girl . . ."

She glanced at him with tears in eyes, but didn't seem to understand Oh Oh's accent. Was it so strange to call her a young girl?

"Help me, I lost my auntie."

Oh Oh had no idea what 'auntie' meant.

"Auntie? What's that? "

"That's *Adaw* in Burmese. She and I got separated."

Okay, Oh Oh reached out to offer his help, but she pulled her arm away. She could tell Oh Oh wasn't town folk, a Hsalon maybe? Hmph! Still I had to help her.

Father's kiosk of traditional Hsalon exhibits was packed with visitors. Showtime was just about to start, so Father was surprised to see Oh Oh come in with a girl, but when he heard the whole story he said, "Don't worry, daughter. Uncle will help you."

Father's words immediately convinced her. They all went to the information centre to make an announcement over the loudspeakers, and soon a woman came. Problem solved. Was this the girl's auntie? She looked very beautiful and very different from sea folk.

Hurrah! The girl smiled and looked happy. Her dimples looked charming when she smiled. "Thanks so much for helping me catch up with my auntie. My name's Cherry. And your name is . . . ?"

"Me? I'm Bida."

"You mean Victor?"

"No, Bida."

"That's hard to pronounce. I'll call you Victor. C'mon, let's go enjoy the show."

Wow! Now it was skirt-girl Cherry's turn to grab Oh Oh by the arm. That was a switch. Okay, then her not wanting Oh Oh to touch her wasn't because I was Hsalon.

"Yay! *Oh! Lu'awhi, nakyi'hsam.*"

* * *

When night fell, people danced around the bonfire. Oh Oh was tired, but there was no place to sleep at home with all the VIPs, so maybe it'd be better to stay at Father's kiosk. While gazing at the fireworks going off from a ship anchored out in the water, he wondered how Cherry was getting on.

"When we got here, all the guesthouses were full. My auntie works for a company. We came with a big group, and we had to stay at the guesthouses there on that side. Coming here by ship was scary, I vomited the whole way. By the time we arrived, I was so tired Auntie left me to get a little sleep. When I woke up, all I saw was the sea. I dashed out to find my auntie, but I got lost. Then I saw you."

Cherry's sweet voice was pleasant. Her auntie could tell Oh Oh was Father's son and seemed to trust me with Cherry. She allowed the two of us to go collect shells and later watch Oh Oh's grandfather participate in the traditional Hsalon boat-carving contest. Ahpo girded his loins and was hollowing a big log.

Three groups competed to three big logs. Cherry clapped her hands and cheered him on. Cherry looked so cute. She liked *wapalok* mixed with sugar, but the creepy-looking *thepalok* disgusted her.

Oh Oh gave Cherry the beautiful shells I hadn't wanted to lend to Father. They made Cherry so happy. Cherry unhooked her necklace to give me as a memento, but I didn't dare accept. City folk were rich, their things were probably too expensive for the likes of Oh Oh.

"Take it, Victor. No problem. It's just a trinket."

"A ticket?"

"Not ticket, *trinket*. Something nice and pretty but inexpensive. I really like this necklace, but it's yours to remember me by. And I'll display your beautiful shells on the bookshelf in our living room."

"Well, then, what will you do with the small shells we collected from the beach?"

"I'll pierce tiny holes to sew onto shirt cuffs and collars for decoration. Things from the sea look precious in Yangon."

Oh Oh didn't understand what Cherry meant by decorating shirts with shells. Of course, the city would be full of things Oh Oh didn't understand. That was nothing unusual. There were also many things in Oh Oh's world they wouldn't understand either. People came all the way here just to experience those things. That's why Father's Hsalon kiosk was packed with visitors. Next door was an art exhibit with paintings of the sea and even a picture of Mother. Before the festival, a visiting artist had painted Mother sitting with her *htamein* (skirt) wrapped high and wearing a string of shells. Father teased her that she looked like a gourd, but she could be a model in town. What was a model? A girl who posed for a painting, said Father.

Where could Cherry be? For sure not at the bonfire. Maybe at the traveling army troupe show? Or taking a nap at her guesthouse? Her ship was leaving tomorrow afternoon, it wouldn't be easy to meet her again once she returned to Yangon. I'd asked her to come to the tents because I wanted to give something to her before she left. Had she forgotten?

* * *

Men came in a hurry and went back in disarray. Boats for Kawthaung and Bokepyin sat anchored midwater, sampans shuttled back and forth. Braving the swarming crowd, which was buzzing like a beehive poked with a stick, Oh Oh went out to the tents. There was no one on the beach, though some foreigners were still taking photos in the tents.

Not long after Oh Oh arrived, Cherry came. She was wearing a blue skirt instead of her yellow skirt. The sky was blue, the water was blue, and now her skirt was blue.

"Hey Victor, Auntie and her group went out boating around the island. You said you'd give me a souvenir..."

"Sure, that's why I asked you here. Just wait a moment." Stripping off my shirt as I spoke, Oh Oh plunged into the water in his shorts. The tents were set up a good way from the surf, but I dived right down and felt my way along the bottom. I'd never had trouble before, but this time I must have been excited. It was hard to get the treasure without breaking it. Careful, careful . . . got it!

Suddenly Oh Oh surfaced and was surprised to see so many people standing outside the tents. Cherry was crying "Help! A boy jumped into the water and never came up... Victor!"

"If he's a Hsalon, don't worry. He's sure to surface," people joked loudly. Cherry must have been frightened to see Oh Oh dive underwater without warning. She probably thought Oh Oh had drowned, but when everyone saw Oh Oh she smiled with tear-streaked eyes.

"What's the fuss? All I did was dive underwater to get you some coral."

"Dear God!"

"The coral was covered with moss and seaweed underwater, so it smells bad. When you get back to town, leave it out to air and it will turn white. It's my souvenir for you. But it's nothing fancy like yours."

Cherry held the coral and laughed heartily. The people crowded around them. When we got to Father's kiosk, he put the coral in a box and tied it up nice and neat with string.

"Victor, I won't forget you. I'll treasure the souvenir you took to get from the water. You Hsalons are a force of nature. I will tell my friends about you, the food here and souvenir you gave me. I've got many photos of you in my camera. Let's not forget each other. I'll come to the next Hsalon Festival. You wait for me, okay?"

That unforgettable day, Oh Oh helped carry their things from the western guesthouse to the ship. Father also left his kiosk to go with us. We went in three sampans to the ship anchored out in the harbour, but visitors were not allowed on board so we had to hurry back to the island. Oh Oh sat watching the ship until the blue-skirt girl leaning on the railing and looking at Bocho Island, vanished from sight. When it had gone, Oh Oh felt empty, my heart was impossibly heavy. What was happening? Why was I so unhappy?

Plastic bags littered the white sand. The kiosks were torn down, boards and bamboo poles piled up. Old Hsalon women wrapped their htameins up high and rolled on the beach to cool off like they always did naturally, but the last remaining foreigners took photos of them. Oh Oh did not like that. What if they thought Hsalons were sand dwellers?

Before the festival, I'd been fresh and alive, but now afterwards I was unhappy. Why did the city girl Cherry make me sad? He still heard her shrill voice, still could see her dimples, her tearful eyes and smiling face. Although I helped Father in body, my mind was far away. My eyes were set on the sea where the ship had gone.

Gradually Bocho Island returned to normal. School reopened and lessons resumed. Father insisted I must try harder at school to become a man of standing in society. He even said he'd send me to study in the big city. To better the lives of the Hsalons, we must be educated.

At school, the kids all talked non-stop about the fun they had at the festival, happy times like they'd never experienced before. Not me, I kept silent. I didn't want to talk to anyone. It was too personal, I didn't want anyone else to know about Cherry. Why was that? Somehow Father seemed to know why I gazed out to sea. All he said was, "You better work hard at your studies if you want to see Cherry again."

* * *

Time passed. The sky still looked blue, the sea was blue too, eh blue-skirt girl? Six years later, after I passed my 10th grade exams at Bokepyin High School and returned to the village, he remembered those wonderful days with the blue-skirt girl.

Father was satisfied with his son's strength. "You shouldn't call yourself Oh Oh any more. That's a baby name. You've passed the 10th Grade, you're no longer a child. Now you're grown-up. Want to race me rowing? Or go running on the west shore?"

When I heard "west shore", I remembered the girl who said she'd return for the Hsalon Festival next year, though there'd been no festival. Fate had tortured us both. Hsalons who got a taste of festive fun had been waiting six years in vain for another festival.

Father vowed to keep his promise to his son who tried hard

at school. Mother didn't like the idea that her son who'd gone to Bokepyin was to be sent off again to Yangon, but Father's decision was law at home.

"My friend U Saw Jet, who used to be based in Wakyun and Thailand, exports fish and prawns. His Annawaso Company is now in Yangon, but if you get a degree and a job with his company you're made for life. As long as the sea exists there'll always be fishery business. A man of the sea should learn the ropes and take it to the international level. If my son advances, my sea products will be more marketable. That's why you must go to Yangon."

Mother had nothing else to add. I had a responsibility toward my three younger brothers and sisters. So it was I got ready to leave the village. While waiting for the boat to Kawthaung from where I'd catch a flight to Yangon, Father said, "When you get there, the company will provide you with food and lodging. Be sure to put your certificates in your bag. Here's a name card. When you get used to life in Yangon, you can go find her. You have your duties just as I have my duties."

I stared at the three-finger-long name-card. Although it had yellowed over six years, it radiated hope. Now I understood why Father had pushed me to try harder. No way would a Hsalon have it easy in Yangon, and now he was sure to face another hurdle with Cherry. He touched the necklace she gave him.

* * *

He was the proverbial country boy in the big city. After a week in Yangon, he still wasn't used to going places by bus. He took one taxi, showing the drivers addresses on name-cards. He had to bring Mae Mae's packages of dried *tin hay* (fish), *nga'lait kyauk u-chauk* (dried ray) and *ye'khu* (jellyfish). He knew from his experience attending school in Bokepyin he probably looked awkward, so he tried not to dress like a yokel.

The taxi stopped right in front of the address on the name-card, a low brick house. He hesitated to go up to the door, but when a plump fair-skinned lady came out he showed her Daw Myat Myat Noe's and Father's name-cards.

44

"Come in, young man, come in! You must be Myat Myat's friend from Makyongalet on Bocho Island. Myat Myat got transferred to Naypyidaw. But Cherry is here. She's doing a computer course, she'll be back soon. Grandma will make you some coffee while you wait."

The living room was cool and fragrant, the floor so shiny clean he dared not set foot on it. The settees were beautiful. He put the parcel of seafood down in the corner and reluctantly took a seat on the settee. Gosh! On the wall were a great many photos that Cherry had taken at the Hsalon Festival. For someone so young, Cherry was good at photography. Hey! Here was a photo of him on a Hsalon boat. The caption underneath read 'Unforgettable Victor'.

My mouth went dry with excitement. All these photos of Father's kiosk and the tents hung up on the wall, did they show Cherry's warm feelings? Here was the coral I'd dived for displayed in a glass case with the caption 'Just like my life'. What could that mean?

"Here's some hot coffee, young man, nice and hot. Oh, you're looking at the photos. As soon as she got back from your Hsalon island, she got busy and put all those shells in glass cases so no one could handle them. Cherry's my younger daughter's child. After she lost both her parents in a car accident she's had no siblings to keep her company, so I've raised her like my own daughter. She's forever going on about the Hsalon Festival. It's been years, but she hasn't stopped talking about it. I stay close and try to listen with interest. She really wanted to go back there the following year, but there was no festival. She'll be happy to see someone from Bocho Island." She smiled as she talked about her beloved granddaughter.

I drank her coffee, but it was tasteless. Sea people might feel full on dried fish and leftover rice, but a cup of coffee hardly satisfied. Having ran out of things to say, I brought out Mae Mae's dried fish and jellyfish.

"I've heard of jellyfish and even eaten it. We never even heard of it when we were children. We'd never been to the sea, never had seafood, but Cherry has relished seafood since the festival.

She often goes to the Thanzay market especially to buy jellyfish and makes salad. It's not bad, nice and crunchy. They say it's good for you, too... Oh, speaking of her."

I heard someone open the gate, then call out *"Ahpwa!* I'm home." Her childhood voice hadn't changed, only now it was clearer and richer. She was wearing trousers and a sweater. "Grandma, who's this? Gosh! It's you, Victor!"

How did she recognise him so quickly? Was it the necklace? She set down her backpack and ran up closer. She was about to grab him by the arm, then stopped. "Victor, how did you get here? What are you up to now? How are your father and mother on Bocho Island? Whenever I get a chance to see a *Rehe'shin* dance from Dawei, I remember you. I want to go back to the festival again. Say something Victor! I haven't heard your accent in so long."

I was almost too excited to speak. I told her I'd attended school in Bokepyin, passed my 10th Grade exams, then went to work for Annawaso Company and wanted to continue studying about trade in sea products. And after that... after that... I wanted to tell her I'd been longing to see her for six whole years. There was a lump in my throat.

"Say, what's in the package?"

"Dried fish I brought."

Her interest shifted to the dried fish. She checked the samples out one by one. "Victor, I'm so happy to see you. We love jellyfish. But where's the *wapalok*? Didn't you bring any?"

"How could I bring it this far? Think about it. If you really want, I'll bring you *thepalok*."

"Victor, you rascal."

Here at last was the real Cherry I'd met on Bocho Island. Ahpwa smiled to see her granddaughter so happy, then went to the kitchen to fix dinner for Cherry and me. Meanwhile I carefully took things out of my backpack.

"Wow! It's beautiful, Victor! What is this creature?"

"It's a *pagé*, also known as a 'seven-colour' rock lobster. It makes a nice room decoration. When Father sent me here to Yangon, I made it myself into a wall hanging. You should put glass over the top for safekeeping."

Cherry was very happy. She stared unblinking at the seven-colour wonder. When they came to the island, it had been out of season.

"You're so clever, a real son of the sea. People can tell a person's origins from how they talk and act. You're heart-to-heart with the sea, you know its secrets so well, you'll be a natural in the sea-product trade." Cherry was eloquent, but I had no idea what she was trying to say. My way of living was nothing special.

She wanted to hang up the 'seven-colour' rock lobster right away, so I helped her. What caption would she write? Under my coral she'd written 'Just like my life'. What would she write now? This time there were no words I didn't understand. She simply wrote 'Sharing my heart'.

Translated from Burmese by U Ye Htut and Alfred Birnbaum

YU YA

Yu Ya (b.1987) is the youngest scion of one of
Myanmar's most famous literary families. The only
woman in Myanmar to hold both a BA and MA in
creative writing, she has won awards in interstate
poetry competitions at township and state level. She
has published more than 40 short stories, poems and
essays for several of the leading literary journals in
Myanmar including *Shwe Amyutae, Thouk Kyar, Yati*
and *Padouk Pwint Thit.* She currently works for BBC
Media Action, contributing to radio dramas on social
and community issues.

SILENCED NIGHT

One of the rising generation of new writers in
Myanmar, Yu Ya is becoming known for her surprising
and eclectic stories. 'Silenced Night' is no different.
The protagonist, typical of Yu Ya's work, is a cat, known
by his human owners as the 'Lanky One'. Through
the Lanky One, Yu Ya illuminates the dangerous
underbelly of life on a Burmese street where grief and
misfortune wait in the shadows. The story is swift, one
sentence thuds into another, with a sparseness crafted
to reveal just enough to keep the reader wondering.
'Silenced Night' is an experiment in style that not all
may desire to see in Myanmar, but
deserves its place.

SILENCED
NIGHT

အသံ့ ည

Meow, meow comes the cry of a cat. A female cat, to be precise. She's been crying for three days, curiously always at midnight. You see, she's a mama-cat who gave birth to a litter. Is she crying because a bigger cat has come and eaten her kittens? Or is she just trying to protect them, to warn those bigger cats to stay away?

* * *

In another house just two doors away, there's a big male cat. So big, in fact, all anyone can say is that's one big cat. Big in size but not fat – it's the length of his body. If you hold his two front paws and stand him up, he's clearly taller than other cats. His owners always show his extraordinary size to visitors, so the tomcat is used to standing upright in front of strangers. Thanks to which, everyone now calls him Lanky.

Lanky was a stray, probably only a year old when he wandered in uninvited, already grown very thin. Maybe nobody fed him. His new owners took pity and decided to adopt him. A good choice, because he's a very tame cat and extremely clean for a male. Three or four times each day, as felines do, he licks his white-striped yellow fur – his very gleaming white and bright yellow coat.

Kids love Lanky. He never scratches or bites, even if they swing him around. Sometimes they put ribbons around his neck or a cap on his head and take photos. He doesn't mind, whatever makes them happy.

The family all love Lanky, even the father who is not so fond of cats. Lanky is a good companion. After staying indoors all day, sleeping in his favourite corner of the house, in the evening he likes to go out and visit the neighbours, then comes back home to say goodnight to the father before he goes to sleep around midnight.

Lanky prefers human food to smelly cat food. He especially loves fried snacks. In the mornings, he likes to eat Chinese breadsticks, samosas or spring rolls that the mother fries up. When he slinks home at night, tired and hungry, he crunches on crisps, fish chips, tofu chips or fried bean paste.

Even so, he eats only when called. At mealtimes, while they prepare his fish or meat, he doesn't nose in, very unusual in a cat. He is, however, a champion mouser. Or rather, he doesn't actually chase mice. Instead, he waits motionless in place for the mouse, then catches it in a single pounce. No mouse can escape him.

And he's very loyal. Once when the grandmother of the family was sick, Lanky didn't leave the house. Which goes against the saying 'cats won't stay around a sick person'. But there he was, waiting patiently with the family every day.

Lanky is obviously very smart. Some even said he's an 'actor cat' because of the knowing way he moves, though his voice is a little too soft for acting. One time the family took him to a movie set. The film crew all loved him and even requested him for the next shoot to play the beloved cat of the main actor and pretend to be dead. When Lanky acted it was so real and sad, they gave him a whole packet of dried shrimp and cat food as payment.

* * *

Then one night, the father waited up for Lanky after his evening walk, but eventually went to bed without setting out his usual late-night crispy snack. In the morning, the mother waited for Lanky to give him his breakfast, but when he still hadn't return, she put aside half a Chinese cruller. A little later, a boy in the street cried out he'd found Lanky. The whole family, mother and father and grandmother, rushed down to find their tomcat lying dead under a car. On a closer look, it was plain to see someone had bashed Lanky on the head, yet he almost managed to drag himself home.

Who could have hurt Lanky? Everyone in the neighbourhood loved him. Then they thought of the new house being built next door. At night, the construction site was guarded by watchmen from who-knows-where. Quite possibly they'd seen Lanky coming every night to visit the mama-cat. Lanky was big and clean, not very plump perhaps but appetising to the men all the same. Who knows how long they'd kept an eye out for Lanky and planned to cook him for dinner? He trusted people, so he couldn't have been very difficult to catch nor could he have cried for help with his soft voice. Even so, he'd somehow crawled off using all his might, but alas home was too far, and he died as in the film.

* * *

The mama-cat's midnight cries continued for many more days. Now everyone knew she was calling for Lanky who would visit no more each night. Her sad cry only ended when her voice gave out. Some might think Lanky was the father of her kittens, but the love between the mama-cat and Lanky was even stranger and sadder. The thing is, Lanky was neutered long ago.

Translated from Burmese by Khin Hnit Thit Oo

LETYAR TUN

Letyar Tun (b.1972) is a writer, translator, photojournalist and former political prisoner. He spent 18 years in prison (14 years on death row) for his political activism. Since his release in 2012, his stories have appeared in multiple journals, his photography has been exhibited in Myanmar and he has spoken on freedom of expression at events across South East Asia. He is a graduate of the 2015 Link the Wor(l)ds literary translation programme and recently gained a scholarship to study at the inaugural School for Interpretation and Translation in Yangon. He currently works for Fojor Media Institute in Yangon.

THE COURT MARTIAL

Advocating a narrative from the other side of the thick green line that ruled Myanmar for fifty years is bound in controversy, and yet despite – or because of – his near twenty year incarceration, Letyar Tun has begun a brief but compelling conversation into the indoctrination of a soldier into the Tatmadaw, where obedience and loyalty to the unit are expected and dissent punished. As the years pass, from basic training to battles in the ethnic states, it is in the capital, Yangon (at the time of the author's own political awakening), where our soldier, Nyo Maung, is compelled to question the authority of those above and accept responsibility for his own in Myanmar's dark past.

THE COURT
MARTIAL

ပတ်ခြီ

The soldiers sat knee to knee in the back of a patrol truck heading into the capital.

"How did the rebels get to Yangon?" asked one of the privates.

"Who are they?" muttered another, nervously picking at his newly starched uniform.

The platoon leader looked at his men. "BCP. Burma Communist Party, that's what we used to call them."

A private next to Nyo Maung poked him in the ribs, interrupting his thoughts. "You really think these guys are BCP?"

Nyo Maung didn't answer, nor did he listen to the chatter as the convoy continued downtown.

* * *

The name 'Burma Communist Party' took Nyo Maung back. All things pass, but not the past. Throughout his thirty years of service in the 'Exalted Military' Tatmadaw, he'd been indoctrinated against the BCP, more than enough to hate them. He'd heard all about their unbelievable atrocities and the bloody purges in the Bago Highlands – or what historians called the "3Ds" of denunciation, dismissal and disposal – where they beat deposed comrades to death with bamboo sticks. And now, so close to retirement, he had to face them once again.

He'd enlisted at 16 and was sent to Basic Military Training School No. 1. He and his fellow cadets were given serial numbers, grouped into companies, and issued uniforms and kit. One morning, the whole troop was wakened by a loud whistle before the usual pre-dawn reveille. The Drill Sergeant huffed over to Nyo Maung and bellowed, "Outside your barracks I found a pile of shit. Which one of you bastards did it?"

Nyo Maung felt the veins in his temples throbbing, his chest pounding. He answered obediently without thinking: "About 3am I heard footsteps outside. I peeked out the window and saw you, sir–" Before he could finish, he felt two hard slaps across his cheeks. He staggered back, knees trembling, though his mind remained clear and calm.

The sergeant leaned in close and spat in Nyo Maung's face. "Now listen up, *missy,* this isn't your mum's house, this is military training! Why would a trainer get up in the middle of the night and shit outside your barracks? So shut your fucking mouth, you lying son of a bitch, got me?"

Nyo Maung stood to attention and shouted as loud as he could, "Yessir!"

The Drill Sergeant backed away and looked across the room. "Fall in and count off!"

The recruits called out their serial numbers one by one. "One, two, three, four…" and the group leader reported back to the sergeant, "Aungzaya Company standing ready for orders, sir."

The Drill Sergeant carried on, "Every one of you crybabies, clean up the shit with your fingers and dump it in the latrine. Do I make myself clear?"

The recruits dared not disobey. Nyo Maung could still smell the shit on his fingers years later.

He remembered the inauguration speech given by the Head of the Military Training School to the new recruits. "If my sons enlisted, I'd tell them a soldier becomes a true man only through the discipline of following orders."

Obedience became the mantra of Nyo Maung's life in the army. Every day his company was drilled to follow orders. Through strict discipline and corporal punishment, they soon learned that obedience was more important than survival or conscience or brotherhood. Order was to be valued above mercy or compassion or any other civilised human quality. Upon completing basic training, he was assigned to the 2nd Infantry Battalion and stationed in the remote Lwal Pan Kuk and Khan Lon regions of northern Shan State to fight alleged communists – ethnic brothers now become enemies.

The brainwashed mind pushed to extremes develops mysterious faculties. Nyo Maung sometimes wondered whether he felt and remembered things more than others. He still had nightmares of places in the hills, villages razed in "scorched earth" manoeuvres. Fogged-in trenches on the Shan Plateau, the smell of blood, the air thick with dust and smoke. From day 1, he was drilled in the "four cuts" – deprive the enemy of food, then finances, then intelligence and finally recruits by driving village elders, women and children from their homes – yet even in his nightmares, even when he was ill and weak, there was a seed of happiness.

* * *

In his first years in Northern Shan State, Nyo Maung was stationed in all three zones: "white" zones under government control and "brown" zones of contested authority, but most of his time he fought in BCP-held "black" zones where any man, woman or child was a potential enemy to be shown no mercy. In black zones, soldiers went "code red" – cruel as sun and fire – though they needed to distance themselves from their targets in order to harden to inhuman purpose.

A commanding officer gave orders to level a village in Lwel Pan Kuk. Nyo Maung's 2nd Platoon blocked off the southern part of the village, while the 1st Platoon herded the villagers north like animals. Suddenly a woman with heavy breasts ran up from the south, and Captain Myint Zaw ordered Nyo Maung to shoot her down.

"My daughter is still in the village!" cried the woman.

"Get down," shouted Nyo Maung.

The Captain repeated his order, "Fire!"

Outright disgust sent a burst of adrenalin rushing through Nyo Maung's body. It happened so very quickly, he hardly realised he'd scrambled out of the foxhole, grabbed the woman and rolled onto the ground. His chest was soaked with her breast milk.

Captain Myint Zaw ran after him, saying, "Nyo Maung, take her to the family barracks. After the operation, you can have her if you want."

And so it was that Nyo Maung married Ma Nan Nwel and made a family.

* * *

The truck halted with a jolt at Sule Pagoda and shook Nyo Maung from his thoughts. In the fading evening light, he saw students the same age as his grown children out in front of Yangon City Hall waving red flags emblazoned with the fighting peacock, wearing red headbands, holding up framed photos of the Father of Independence, General Aung San.

The whole squad shuffled into a line formation, linking arms shoulder to shoulder. They aimed their loaded guns at the students before them. Nyo Maung didn't like it, the targets were too close. The enemy was unarmed; for sure they weren't members of the Burma Communist Party. Just maybe he could shoot above their heads in the dark and no one would know. He didn't need any more nightmares so close to retirement.

His prayers, however, went unheard. At a secret signal, the army truck headlights switched on full beam. The students' faces went white, squinting in the glare, perhaps realising their fate. Staring at each other in silence, the students wondered when the soldiers would shoot and the soldiers waited for orders to do so. A matter of seconds, but to Nyo Maung it was a lifetime. Until a bird chirped, then "Fire!" resounded – and the soldiers mowed down the students.

* * *

After several months in Insein Prison, Nyo Maung was summoned out of his cell and handed a sheaf of typed papers detailing his criminal breach of military code: disobeying a superior's command in the field. He barely glanced at the indictment before signing his name on the last page. He didn't care what it said, he just wanted to know what they'd do to him now.

As he walked into the courtroom, he told himself, "I don't kill innocent people. If I'd pulled the trigger, their faces would haunt me. I was taught to obey orders and eliminate targets, but I've changed, I'm no longer the young recruit I was. I've seen too many targets who weren't enemies. I disobeyed orders, I failed the Tatmadaw, but had I obeyed I'd have failed myself. What is disobedience? Disobeying the rules to appease myself may be a crime, but failing to obey my conscience only gives me nightmares."

The ceiling fans whirred in a slow rhythm. Mould crept into the corners of the whitewashed walls. The wide windows looked out onto the barren prison yard. Nyo Maung was marched up to a low, wooden dock flanked by two long tables. His feet scuffed the broken floor tiles, echoing angrily through the colonial hall. Before the Burma Socialist Program Party emblem sat three court martial judges – two majors and a colonel – neat and robotic in their crisp green uniforms, with pommaded hair, wire-rimmed glasses and gold stars on their shoulders. Nyo Maung knew obedience had raised them in the ranks to where they could sentence any soldier to death.

Translated from Burmese by the author

JUNE NILIAN SANG

June Nilian Sang (b.1988) is an ethnic Chin writer and editor, born in Thantlang, Northern Chin State. Graduating with a BA in English from Kalaymyo University, he moved to India after the 2007 Saffron Revolution, returning to Myanmar in 2012. He has held several positions at Lai Hakha language journals, including online editor of the *Chinland Post*, Chief Editor of the *Chin Times* and Executive Editor of the *Chin Digest*. He speaks five languages: Lai Hakha, Lai Falam, Mizo, English and Burmese. He writes under the pen name 'Salai JNS'.

TAKEAWAY BRIDE

The romanticism of youth and love are a common trope in the Burmese-language literary cannon, where trials of strength and cunning must be overcome before the couple can be reunited. Here, June Nilian Sang inserts a more pernicious ordeal all too common in his Chin community, where women are 'sold' to bachelors overseas, and the price of the bride supports those she has left behind. 'Takeaway Bride', originally written in the Lai Hakha language, poignantly conveys the experience of both the boy, Ta Biak, and the girl, Nu Bwai as they struggle to admit what the other means to them and to accept how quickly what they have can slip away. In doing so June Nilian Sang swings between the angst of the individual desire and submission to the needs of the family before this ordeal of love is finally resolved.

TAKEAWAY
BRIDE

Parcel Maw Ka Chuahchan Si Hnga

Whenever he has time on his hands, Ta Biak likes to read. His favourite place is a chair in the corner of the living room. This evening, he has already spent a couple of hours with a book, but right now something is bothering him. He can hear his sisters gossiping in the kitchen. Normally he wouldn't listen to them, but they're talking about Nu Bwai and a cousin of hers who has just returned from America. At the mention of Nu Bwai's name, he leans over in his chair to hear better. If his sisters knew Ta Biak was eavesdropping, they'd have talked more quietly, not wanting to upset him. But they carry on, unaware that he's hanging onto their every word. This cousin, Cung Cung, they say, came to Nu Bwai's house last night and proposed to her. He even wants her to go live with him in America.

* * *

Nu Bwai and Ta Biak are neighbours. They've been like sister and brother since childhood. They went to school together and played near each other's houses every evening. After high school they attended different universities, but the special bond between them didn't diminish. Come holiday breaks, the first place Ta Biak went was to Nu Bwai's house. Nu Bwai is one of the prettiest girls in the district; some boys even think she looks like a Korean actress they

59

might see on television. Neighbours and friends assumed Ta Biak and Nu Bwai were a couple, they spent so much time together. But no, despite their intimacy, neither of them has spoken words to break the unconscious barrier of innocence that grew between them over the years.

Cung Cung didn't know or care. The first time he told Nu Bwai he liked her, he was preparing to leave Chin State for Malaysia, where there were jobs and money. Nu Bwai wasn't interested. She told him she'd just graduated and had to concentrate on further studies. Perhaps she also knew then she just wanted to be with Ta Biak.

* * *

Ta Biak is nervous. He lays his book on the sidetable and decides to go for a walk to clear his head. But when he gets to the front door he hesitates. He doesn't know what to do. He starts to doubt what he's overheard. Did Cung Cung really propose to Nu Bwai? And did she say yes? He can't stay shut up indoors anymore, it is stifling. He sits under a tree in the garden. He wants answers, but whom should he ask? His sisters had said Nu Bwai's mother had arranged it, but he can't go to her. There's only one person who can tell him the truth: Nu Bwai herself. He must walk to her house that very night.

* * *

"Is Nu Bwai in, Auntie?" asks Ta Biak.

"Yes, she's here," replies Nu Bwai's mother, Parte. "Come in, son."

Nu Bwai is washing dishes in the kitchen and hears Ta Biak talking to her mother. "Wait. I'll be there in a minute."

At the sound of her voice, Ta Biak's heart beats faster. How can he ask her about last night? What if she gets angry? Parte invites him in, but he doesn't know what to say. Luckily, Parte soon leaves for choir practice at church, leaving them alone. Minutes later, Nu Bwai comes and sits next to him. Seeing Ta

Biak's face, she knows there's something wrong.

"Are you okay, Ta Biak?" she asks. "Why do you look so sad?"

Ta Biak is shy, speechless. Perhaps he's silent because the words he wants to say are no longer innocent. He tries to speak, to ask her, but no sooner he has found the courage than Nu Bwai interrupts him. She's always been a chatterbox. Ta Biak starts to think perhaps Nu Bwai doesn't know about Cung Cung. Just maybe, he starts to hope, Parte hasn't told her yet.

Biting his lip hard, he whispers, "Nu Bwai."

"Yes."

Again, her voice pounds on his heart. All he can think to say is, "What did you do today?"

Nu Bwai knows there's something wrong with Ta Biak. His awkward expression, his unusual questions. She tries not to laugh, but doesn't really understand. The evening wears on until Parte returns from church and Ta Biak goes home, depressed at having failed to confirm his sisters' gossip.

With Ta Biak gone, Parte sits next to her daughter. She hasn't told Nu Bwai yet about Cung Cung's visit, but she can't wait forever. "My daughter, your father is dead, I'm running the shop alone, and it's hard work. Your brother's school fees are getting more expensive every year. You marrying Cung Cung is the only answer," she explains. "Will you say yes?"

Nu Bwai is stunned. Now she understands why Ta Biak was so sad. Since her father died, Nu Bwai has done everything her mother has asked, but to marry Cung Cung? How can she say yes? "But we're not even a couple," she protests.

"Not everyone who marries loves each other at the beginning," her mother explains, "but many arranged marriages are blessed. It is every mother's wish to see her daughter get married to a good man and live a life of comfort. That's all I want for you."

Nu Bwai recalls Cung Cung's face and wonders how she could possibly go with him. "Let's talk about this later, mum," she says in frustration and disappears into her bedroom.

* * *

It's nearly midnight, but Ta Biak can't sleep. He's annoyed with himself, why didn't he find the courage to ask her? Lying in bed, he speaks to Nu Bwai as if she were next to him. "It's too late, Nu Bwai. I should have told you earlier how I felt. But now it's too late."

There's no point in trying to sleep now. Ta Biak steals out of the house, careful not to wake his family. The village is quiet at midnight, the sky free of clouds, the moon shining on him. He sits on a wooden bench opposite his house and taps at his mobile phone looking for his favourite love song, then turns down the volume so only he can hear Sui Tha Par's voice.

"If you want me to be with you, you should say I love you. Come to me through my heart's door. It opens for you alone. By tomorrow, I will be gone far away with somone I don't love and leave the one who really loves me. Give me your hand before it's too late."

Listening, Ta Biak wonders, "Does Nu Bwai sing the same words for me?"

He can't bear the thought of Nu Bwai leaving without letting her know. Butterflies in his stomach, he walks to her house anyway and sits under a large tree out front. It hurts him to remember how they use to play under this tree when they were young.

* * *

Ta Biak is not the only one in the village who can't sleep; but it's too late for Nu Bwai to leave her house. Instead, she stares at the night sky from her bedroom window and thinks. Not about Cung Cung, but of Ta Biak. How could she leave him and go to America with someone she hardly knows and doesn't love? The moon is so bright tonight, from her window she can see the tree where she and Ta Biak played as children – only tonight she also sees a figure. At first, she thinks it might be a thief. Who else would be out at this hour? But quickly she sees the shadow for who it really is. Just as Ta Biak did, she tiptoes downstairs, opens the front door, and whispers as loud as she dares, "Ta Biak."

Too dark to see who's calling so late at night, Ta Biak hides behind the tree. Nu Bwai calls his name again, this time louder, and he recognises her voice. He peers around the tree and sees her. "What are you doing?" he hisses. "It's midnight!"

She turns the question back to him. "Well, what about you?"

"I…" Again he has no words.

The night is not dark enough to hide the sadness in their faces, nor does it obscure the whites of their eyes now flush with the truth. Ta Biak emerges from behind the tree and walks over to her. The words caught in his throat begin to tumble out, words trapped inside him since he was a young boy.

"I haven't thought of anything else since I heard the news. I've wanted to tell you how I felt for a long time now, but I waited too long. I never thought someone else would come, and now it's too late."

Tears roll down Nu Bwai's blushing cheeks.

"Why are you crying?" asks Ta Biak.

Nu Bwai has no reply. She throws herself forward and embraces him.

"It's never too late," she tells him. "Even though you never said anything, I've always known. I'll say no to Cung Cung and anybody else who asks me. I only want to be with you."

Holding each other tightly, they wonder how they can make this possible. They agree to explain everything to Nu Bwai's mother in the morning.

Neither of them sleep that night, both wondering if Parte will give her blessing.

When the sun rises, Ta Biak returns once again to Nu Bwai's house. Driven by the hope Nu Bwai has given him, he knocks on the front door and asks, "Auntie, may I talk with you?"

"Of course, Ta Biak."

Parte shows Ta Biak into the living room and sits down next to him. "What is so important that brings you here so early?"

Nu Bwai enters from another room and sits close to Ta Biak.

"Auntie, you know Nu Bwai and I have been like brother and sister since we were children. But we're not children anymore. I know someone wants to take her far away from here, from me. I simply can't let that happen, and I know Nu Bwai feels the same way."

Dumbfounded, Parte glances at Nu Bwai out of the corner of her eye, then calls her by her birth name, as only a mother can. "Bwai Zing!"

Nu Bwai falls off the chair onto her knees. "Forgive me mother," she cries. "Ta Biak is more than just a brother to me. I can't leave him to go live in a different country."

Her mother pauses, unsure of what to say. The room is silent. Parte thinks, but only for a moment, then reaches down and hugs her daughter.

She whispers to Nu Bwai. "Don't cry, my daughter. I would never have arranged the marriage between you and Cung Cung had I known."

Parte then turns to Ta Biak. "And you, Ta Biak, please don't be upset. I never knew you were in love with my daughter."

Ta Biak kneels down in front of Parte, and with Nu Bwai by his side, tightly clasps Parte's outstretched hand.

Translated from Lai Hakha to Burmese by Rev. Taan Mang,
and from Burmese to English by Aung Min Khant

MYINT WIN HLAING

Myint Win Hlaing (b.1981) is an ethnic Rakhine writer and teacher born in Pan Ni La village, Rakhine State. He is a leading member of an influential Rakhine literature circle organising talks and live literature events for his remote community. He has published short stories both in Burmese, in *Shwe Amyutae* and *Yote Shin Tay Kabyar* magazines, and in the Rakhine language in *Rakhine Journal*. He writes under the pen name Green Maung.

THE POISONED FUTURE

In perhaps the unhappiest tale in this anthology, two societies collide, as Lon Lon Chaw, pregnant and unmarried, is cast out of the family only to be embraced on the fringes of the river community. As we follow Lon Lon Chaw's miserable journey to motherhood, Myint Win Hlaing toys with our expectations, burrowing into all that is good and bad within us. Flitting, in turns, from the macabre to the salacious, 'The Poisoned Future', originally written in the Rakhine language, nevertheless shines a much needed light into a darkened corner of Myanmar society.

THE POISONED FUTURE

အဆိပ်သင့် အနာဂတ်

The horizon grows dark in all directions. Thick rain clouds, drifting in southerly winds, cover the sky as evening falls and the farmers head home. To the north of town is a small hill, verdant with giant banyans, tamarinds and parrot trees that boast clusters of red-beaked flowers in April. Under the trees hide dirt graves and whitewashed tombs overgrown in weeds. Through the surrounding bush a young man shoulders something rolled in a frayed palm-leaf mat. Ahead of him walk three other men carrying a mattock, a hoe and bottles of water and homebrew. Together, the four men scout for a bare patch of ground amid the dirty rags, charred bamboo and plastic throwaways.

"In the end, all of mankind must rest here. Us too one day. You're not afraid are you?" the young man Soe Paing asks the others.

He takes the mattock and begins to dig into the hard ground. Soe Paing is the oldest of the four. He dropped out of high school after his father died, to support the family by working at his uncle's bicycle and trishaw repair shop while his friends attended university in the state capital, Sittwe. As the eldest of the young villagers, he's also in charge of all joyous and sombre occasions from weddings to funerals.

"The only difference between the town and here is life and death," Soe Paing continues, wielding the hoe to widen the hole.

"Here it doesn't matter if you're rich or poor."

"No, you're wrong," counters Maung Maung. "Look over there, the rich rest in tombs, while the poor sleep under mounds of earth."

It starts to rain, and the digging gets messy as the water begins to rise.

"Myo Lin, go fetch that scoop over by that tomb there and bail out the water will you?"

"Okay, Ko Soe Paing, just let me drink up," says Myo Lin, draining his cup.

While Myo Lin and Soe Paing work, Bo Aung sits beside the mat nursing the bottle of liquor. "Like the saying goes, 'where walks an ill-fated woman, rain follows'. This baby was unlucky. Even her human birth didn't guarantee her a father or a long life. The rain isn't stopping. She really does make trouble for others." Bo Aung takes another swig from the bottle while talking to himself.

Myo Lin throws down the scoop and shouts at Bo Aung. "If you're going to drink, at least mind the corpse. I can hear the dogs howling in the woods. Besides, the girl wasn't so ill-fated. In the Lord Buddha's teachings I've read, it says *Manusatta bavo dullabo* – 'Being born a human is precious.' Easier it is for a needle from the heavens to strike a needle on earth than to be born in the human realm. If you're born human, it means you've already achieved a higher life than before. Long life or short, that's different though. That's the result of your own doings in life."

Ill-fated or not, a woman had borne her, nine months in the womb. And despite poverty, sympathetic souls took care of her for three months thereafter. Surely many babies had the good fortune to be born human like her yet did not survive; just as many unborn babies were cruelly aborted by unmotherly mothers.

* * *

After her parents died, Lon Lon Chaw moved in with her aunt. Her aunt Daw Than Mya ran a liquor joint and had a reputation in the village for brewing alcohol so strong it could burst into flames. Daw Than Mya's husband drinks the stuff all day, and walks around with red eyes and swollen cheeks.

Lon Lon Chaw had to feed pigs in the sty behind the house and clean the yard as well as work as a waitress in the liquor joint. She was not as attractive as her name 'curvy beauty' implied, though healthy with a round bottom, a tiny waist, pointed breasts and brown skin; local men thought she walked like a young mare and never tired of watching her. Because of her age she could meet customers far more easily than younger teenage girls. Her looks and the fashionable – but cheap – dresses she wore made men hungry, though normally they wouldn't eat when drinking.

After she started working there, the liquor joint got busier than ever, and everyone knew why. She served all the men equally, young or old, and was so polite and sweet that Daw Than Mya's liquor trade grew and grew. Every teacher, clerk and trishaw driver in the village called her by name, Lon Lon.

One customer, retired civil servant U Ba San came in regularly, always at the same time of day. "I drink, not because I like alcohol," he told his drinking buddies, "but as medicine for my cardiovascular disease."

His wife had already passed away and his adult children lived on their own, so U Ba San was free and single. A good talker, he enjoyed living without rules and obligations. Only rarely, on unavoidable social and religious occasions, did he go to temple. Behind his back the villagers called him an old ox who liked to eat tender grass.

His oldest son warned him, "Father, you really should consider your age and take solace in religion." But U Ba San just shouted back, "I didn't raise you to preach to me. I trust my own conscience. Get out!" After that, his children didn't dare tell him what other people were saying.

"A woman's beauty does not belong to her alone. It's meant to be shared. Before one dies, one should savour it as much as possible. Who knows if there'll be a next life?" U Ba San told his friends, raising his glass and laughing.

* * *

"Hey, have you heard?"

"Heard what? The girl from the liquor joint?"

"Yes, her. She's pregnant."

The gossip spread through the village to the liquor house. One by one the customers stayed away. Not even U Ba San came, despite having to drink regularly for his health problems.

Daw Than Mya couldn't take it anymore and shouted at Lon Lon Chaw. "Look what you've gone and done, bitch! My business, my reputation is ruined. I want you gone, right now!"

"You're right. It's my fault. Curse me, beat me," said Lon Lon Chaw.

"What did you say? *Now* you see it's your fault, do you? Why couldn't you see that from the start? Get out of here right this minute!" Daw Than Mya grabbed Lon Lon Chaw by the arm and dragged her out of the house.

"Hey, Than Mya, that's enough. Scold her if you must, but don't beat her," said her husband, trying to calm her down. "This girl's your own niece."

"Mind your own business. She's not my niece, she's a whore." Daw Than Mya screamed and swore at Lon Lon Chaw so loudly you could hear her ten houses away.

"I'd like to crush you to a pulp. Get out! I don't want to see your damned face ever again."

Lon Lon Chaw left her aunt's house with nothing but her clothes. With nowhere to go, she pictured her parents. "Mum, Dad, help me, I'm in trouble," she murmured to herself.

Her steps took her to the Kissapa River, where the relentless current had worn away the trees and rocks below a small cliff. A good place to kill myself, she thought. She stood on the precipice, thinking randomly with eyes closed, tears streaming down her cheeks. An orphan herself, she felt only sadness for the unborn child inside her and didn't want the child to pay for the mistakes she had made in her life. Closing her eyes even tighter, Lon Lon Chaw put her palms together and began to chant a prayer.

"Hey, girl!"

A rough hand grabbed Lon Lon Chaw's blouse from behind, and both of them fell backwards.

"What are you doing, girl? It's dangerous here, go home!" gasped an old woman, hugging her tightly.

"I don't have a home to go to. This is my only choice. Don't hold me back me, grandma."

"Oh, it's you. Aren't you the girl from Than Mya's place?"

"Yes, that's me, grandma." Lon Lon Chaw confided.

"Oh Lord, Lord, Lord, it always happens like this," mumbled the old woman. "Come stay with me, my granddaughter. Don't you worry, it's right and just to give a hand to one in trouble. And also I get a companion."

"Can I really stay with you, grandma? I'm with child, so it's not just me."

"Then I'll help you when it's time to deliver your baby. When I go hungry, you'll go hungry too, but when I have food, so will you... that's all," said the old woman, taking Lon Lon Chaw's hand to lead her home.

The old woman, Daw Mae Kya had lived alone in a tiny hut at the far edge of the village for more than fifty of her seventy years. With neither family nor relatives, hers was a hard and frugal life. She scraped up land crabs, she netted fish, she gathered leaves for salad. She survived.

* * *

Lon Lon Chaw, alone in the hut while the old woman went out to forage for firewood, groaned in agony. She knew there were people all around, but didn't dare ask for help. The child was moving, struggling. Hearing the painful cries, a woman entered the hut and was shocked to see Lon Lon Chaw lapsing into unconsciousness. She called the other neighbour women, who came running to the hut. One of them took pity on Lon Lon Chaw. "We can't just sit here, we have to take her to hospital."

"Hospital? With no money? Impossible! We have to pay for everything at the hospital, even cotton wool."

"We have no choice, we've got to take her there."

"Just because we don't have money, should we just let her die?"

The neighbours argued until they reached a decision. Wrapping Lon Lon Chaw in a hammock, they carried her to the hospital. The doctor on duty, U Maung Gyi, had just been posted to the village. He quickly examined the girl before registering her.

"Patient's name?"

"Lon Lon Chaw, Doctor," answered a woman, arms folded across her chest.

"Husband's name?"

No one spoke.

Dr Maung Gyi asked again, "Who is the husband?"

"She has no husband," replied the same woman.

"And her parents?"

"Deceased. The old woman Daw Mae Kya adopted her."

"*Tsk, tsk.* Bring her in to the operating room," said the doctor, setting down his ballpoint pen on the registry.

After a long labour, Lon Lon Chaw gave birth to a baby girl. The doctor himself took on the charges for her medical treatment, and even bought her food and vitamins. In the recovery room, he told Lon Lon Chaw, "Thanks to you, this baby has been given a chance to be born a human. I do admire your courage. Please let me know if you have any problems."

"Thank you, doctor, I'm so grateful. I won't forget your help."

* * *

The four young men have dug the hole as deep as they can. As Soe Paing picks up the rolled mat and places it in the grave, Bo Aung stops him.

"Wait, Ko Soe Paing. Not just yet."

"What is it, Bo Aung? We're running out of time, it's already dark."

"We haven't seen the baby yet. Everyone knew Lon Lon Chaw was pregnant, but we still don't know who the father was. If we take a peek, maybe we can guess, heh, heh."

"No, that's not the way, Bo Aung. Everything's already over and done with."

Turning to Soe Paing, he says, "Already done? I don't care what's right or wrong, I want to know."

Bo Aung unrolls the cursed mat anyway. The baby is wrapped in a thin blanket. He takes a long look at the tiny body, but in the darkness under the black rain clouds, not a dim sliver of light reaches the face of the baby.

Translated from Rakhine to Burmese by Dr San Hla Kyaw,
and from Burmese to English by Letyar Tun

MAW MA THAE

Maw Ma Thae (b. 1988) is an ethnic Kayah, born in Demawso Township, Kayah State. She is an active member of the once outlawed Kayah Nationalities Literacy and Culture Committee, assisting in ongoing community projects promoting Kayah literature and mother-tongue-based education.

THE LOVE OF KA NYA MAW

Modern fiction has a deep, narrative debt in the now fading tradition of oral storytelling. In 'The Love of Ka Nya Maw', originally written in the Kayah Li language, the authority and status of these early epics is humbly evoked by Maw Ma Thae in a blend of the old and the modern. The protagonist, the similarly named Ma Thae, learns to overcome her fear of the big city through the friendship of a man from home. But when she returns to her village in Kayah State, doubts emerge and she searches for answers in the odyssey of the legendary Kayah Prince Suu Reh and his wife, the eponymous Ka Nya Maw.

THE LOVE OF KA NYA MAW

တၟ်ၟၟၟၟ ၟၟၟၟ

I heard a cock crowing again in the distance and tried to open my eyes. Sunlight filtered through the woven bamboo wall. When I opened the window, it was already getting bright. Mum must have got up earlier than me, but hadn't woken me because I'd been writing on my computer late into the night.

After about five minutes, I heard a motorcycle pull up in front of the house and someone call out my name. "Maw Thae, Maw Thae, are you home?"

Wondering what was going on, I hurried out down the steps before I recognised my friend.

"Maw Thae, you have to go to Yangon tomorrow. You'd better pack your things."

"Yangon? What for?"

"To attend a seminar in Kayah literature, so you can teach a children's course. Another teacher, our Sayama will go with you. Well, gotta run," he said, then drove off.

I was upset that I had to go to Yangon, and so suddenly. I'd never been to Yangon before. I was nervous and a bit frightened. "Okay, for the sake of our people, I'll go with Sayama." I tried to rally.

The next day, Sayama and I boarded the bus with our bags. It was fun at first, but as the hours wore on I began to feel stiff. Some passengers suffered from motion sickness and vomited repeatedly. I didn't feel nauseous, though my back ached. Yet even so, by evening I grew drowsy.

"Be careful with your purse or someone might snatch it," Sayama warned me.

I fell asleep holding my purse close to my chest until hours later, when the driver shouted "Last stop!" and everyone got off. I was still half-asleep, so Sayama had to give me a little nudge. I quickly grabbed my bag, then Sayama hailed a taxi to the hostel, not far from the seminar venue, where we would be staying with many others.

The seminar ran from six in the morning to four in the afternoon, which left our evenings free, but since most of us had never been to a big city like Yangon before, we were too afraid to go out sightseeing. Instead, we stayed at the hostel playing guitar and singing songs. Only after a week of training did I feel brave enough to walk around. One evening, when I went to a nearby shop to buy some snacks, a young man eyeing me from half a block away started following me back to the hostel. Trembling in fear, I tried to stay calm and keep walking, my shaky steps barely touching the ground.

"Hey, Kayah girl!" he called out, coming closer and closer. "Don't be afraid, I'm an okay guy."

I relaxed a little, enough to turn and yell at him. "Why are you following me?"

"You're Kayah, aren't you? I hear you singing lovely Kayah songs every evening," he replied.

After that, we became friends. He lived near our hostel, so we'd go out for snacks together. I was his first Kayah friend. But the seminar was nearly over. His face furrowed in sadness when I told him I'd be going back to my village. He insisted I see more of Yangon before I left, so those final days he took me to Inya Lake, Sein Gayha Shopping Centre and the Ethnic Nationalities Village.

"When you're back in your village, you won't forget me, will you?" he asked.

"Of course not, but before I go, can I ask you a question? What's your ethnicity?"

"I'm Kayah," he replied.

I was astonished. "Then why do you talk to me in Burmese?"

"Well, it's just that… I've lived in Yangon since I was a child, so I can't speak Kayah, only Burmese. But you can call me by my Kayah name, Khu Rhe."

When the time came to leave Yangon, Khu Rhe asked, "If I to come Kayah State, will you show me around?"

"Of course," I replied eagerly.

I gave him my phone number just before boarding the bus. As we zoomed away, I looked back and saw him waving. Tears came to my eyes, and for the first time I realised I didn't want to leave him behind.

* * *

After about three months, in the early spring when there wasn't much farm work to do, some people went on little trips to different places. I was thinking about going somewhere myself when the phone rang.

"Sis, you're wanted on the phone," my younger brother called out.

I picked up the phone wondering who it could be and was happy to hear a familiar voice on the other end. I really hadn't expected Khu Rhe would call me.

"I'd like very much to come and see you," he said.

"Please do."

"I've missed you…" he continued, but I couldn't say a word.

Two or three days later was Deemawso town market day. I left home without eating, and had just ordered rice and sausage at a lunch stall when I saw a young man who looked very much like Khu Rhe in the crowd. I gulped down my food and paid the bill, but lost sight of him. I looked for him all over until I was so tired I had to sit down under a tree to rest my sore legs. After a while, who should walk up but the same young man. It really was Khu Rhe. We looked at each other in surprise. He greeted me *Mingalaba!* in Burmese and I replied with a Kayah *De rhe ban ne!* And when he reached out to me, I felt such an excited thrill I quickly withdrew my hand.

"What luck!" he said. "I was thinking about visiting you after the market. I didn't expect to meet you here. It's really wonderful to see you." The two of us wandered around the market a while, then Khu Rhe said, "Let's go somewhere else."

"How about the seven-tier lakes?" I suggested.

"I'd love to," he replied. "I've never heard of them."

So we bought some snacks and went to the first of the seven-tier lakes. Sitting together on the shore, Khu Rhe said, "This lake is really beautiful. The mountains on both sides, trees all around so natural and green. I can't describe it, I have to take a photograph."

"Yes, it's pretty as a picture here," I agreed.

"But why are they called the seven-tier lakes?" he asked.

"Well, legend has it that originally there was one lake that divided into seven," I explained. "This one is called Lake Pobya."

"Could you tell me the story?"

* * *

Once upon a time, there was a Prince by the name of Suu Reh. One day, while hunting in the woods, he happened upon the goddess Ka Nya Maw and her sisters bathing in a lake. It was love at first sight. He felt such a great love for Ka Nya Maw, the youngest of the seven, and desired so much to live with her that he stole her robe and hid it. After bathing, the other goddesses got dressed, but Ka Nya Maw couldn't find her things. "Did any of you see my robe?" she asked her sisters.

"No," the others answered in unison. They all helped search long and hard, but to no avail. "It'll be getting dark soon, we must fly home now," they said, ascending to the heavens.

Ka Nya Maw, left all alone, started to cry, when just then the Prince came out of hiding carrying her clothes.

"Would you please give back my robe?" Ka Nya Maw pleaded.

"Certainly, but only if you come live with me," demanded Prince Suu Reh.

"But you're a human and I'm a goddess. We can never live together, I can't come with you."

Still the Prince insisted, so Ka Nya Maw had no choice but to go along to his country. In time, true love blossomed between them and a son was born.

In the Prince's country, there was a young woman who was infatuated with the Prince, a woman whose love he didn't requite. When the Prince came back to his country with his new bride, the woman felt a deep hatred towards Ka Nya Maw and planned to kill her.

There came a time when the country was invaded by enemy troops and so the King sent the Prince to fight the enemies, for the Prince was smart with immense courage. Seizing the opportunity, the cunning woman went to the King and said, "In order to quell the invaders and maintain peace in the country, we must make a sacrificial offering to the god Byadaye." The King took up the suggestion and prepared to offer the blood of a sacrificial victim, but the despicable woman addressed the King again, "The blood offered to Byadaye must be pure and holy. Only the blood of Ka Nya Maw Dwe Mei Naw will satisfy the god's appetite."

Hearing that the only goddess in the country, Ka Nya Maw, was to be executed by royal order, her mother-in-law the Queen hurried to her and said, "Go home, my daughter. The King is going to kill you."

But Ka Nya Maw merely cried at the thought of abandoning her husband and son, and refused to leave. The time came for her to be executed and the Queen insisted that she fly away.

"Please put a large bowl in the doorway," Ka Nya Maw told the Queen, while cuddling her baby son to her breast.

After doing as instructed, the Queen returned and repeated, "Now please, you must go home."

Ka Nya Maw came out and squeezed some milk from her breast into the bowl. "Be quick, my daughter, be quick," said the Queen worriedly.

Hesitantly, Ka Nya Maw Dwe Mei Naw rose to the heavens. But not before meeting a monk and giving him a ring, saying "Please deliver this to my husband."

After some time, the Prince returned from the battlefield. Whereupon the monk came to give him the ring and a herbal potion. "If ever you encounter danger, difficulties or problems, this cure will protect you," said the monk.

When the Prince found his wife missing, he immediately left the palace to look for her. He encountered a huge serpent and killed it. He traversed a field of grass blades sharp as knives. He swam across the mighty Salween River. Exhausted from his journey, the Prince rested under a big tree in whose branches he heard birds singing.

"There's going to be a ceremony tomorrow. The goddess Ka Nya Maw will have her hair washed to cleanse the sin of living with the humans," chirped one of the birds. "Let's go and enjoy the feast!"

Overhearing this, the Prince changed himself into an ant and climbed up the tree to grab onto the feathers of one of the birds, who then swiftly flew up and perched on the wall of the heavenly kingdom just as Ka Nya Maw's six elder sisters were fetching water from a pool. He secretly threw the ring into an earthen pot carried by the sixth goddess, so when they poured the water, the ring dropped out with a clink.

When the sixth goddess told their Lord Father, he said, "Who could have put the ring into the pot? There must be a human here!"

Seeing the ring, however, the youngest goddess knew the Prince had come after her and begged, "Father, please let my husband in."

"It's the seventh day of ablutions," he pronounced. "You can no longer be with your husband."

The goddess grew despondent and pleaded to be allowed to live with her husband. The Lord Father then said, "My daughter, your husband is surely very brave, but I must test his strength and intelligence."

Whereupon the Prince was summoned in. First, he had the Prince shoot at a target with bow and arrow, a simple task for him. Second, he ordered him to lift a heavy boulder, which he lifted with his enormous strength as easily as if it were a wad of cotton. Last, the Lord Father asked his seven daughters to poke a finger through holes in a wall and ordered the Prince to determine which finger belonged to the youngest goddess. Their fingers were all so delicate and beautiful it was very difficult for him to tell them apart, but when he saw a fly hovering over one of the fingers he knew that it had to be Ka Nya Maw's.

The Lord Father said, "You're talented and clever. You are worthy to claim my daughter as your wife." And so the Prince and Goddess lived happily ever after.

* * *

No sooner had I finished than Khu Rhe told me, "That was a really nice story. I enjoyed it very much," then reached over and took my hand again. "I will love you just like the Prince loved Ka Nya Maw and find you wherever you go."

I was thrilled to hear his words, but after many happy days together Khu Rhe went back to Yangon and I haven't spoken to him since, nor has he contacted me. I tried to call, but his phone doesn't work. Weary and worried, I have been waiting and waiting for him to find me again. Months have gone by, yet still I hope, like Ka Nya Maw. Where are you, Khu Rhe?

Translated from Kayah Li to Burmese anonymously,
and from Burmese to English by Dr Mirror (Taunggyi)

SAN LIN TUN

San Lin Tun (b.1974) is a writer born in Yangon from Mon-Burmese parents. A graduate of the 2015 Link the Wor(l)ds literary translation programme, his fiction has appeared in numerous local and international publications including the *New Asian Writing Anthology*. He is the author of ten books in English, including the short novel *Walking Down an Old Literary Road* (Mudita Books, 2008) and the short-story collection *A Classic Night at Café Blues and Other Stories* (Mudita Books, 2010). His latest book, a collection of essays entitled *Reading a George Orwell Novel in a Myanmar Teashop* was published in 2016.

AN OVERHEATED HEART

While many of San Lin Tun's stories explore the process of writing, the elaborate paths taken and those we encounter on them, 'An Overheated Heart' also alludes to those singular moments in our lives where the chance to escape can give us a reason to return. Here, the protagonist Lin Yaung is beguiled by the young woman, Naw Phawl Wah. He sets out to impart his knowledge of writing to a small class of students – but along the way the teacher–student dynamics are overthrown and, as he slides into a morass of doubt and suspicion, he finds himself leaning on a most unexpected shoulder.

AN OVERHEATED
HEART

ရင်ခွင်ဝေးဝေး

Lin Yaung was bored with his life. Bored and lonely. And in his loneliness, he often reflected, as he did right now, on the causes and implications of this *loca,* the meaning and essence of life as set forth in *Abhidhamm* philosophy. Of course, he never arrived at any simple answer to these complex questions, but he enjoyed trying. Not that he was a Socrates or an Aristotle, but he did believe he ought to be able to decide the course of his own life.

Seeing thinking to be his only skill, he'd spent much of his life in pursuit of education while his friends sought property. They were now financially secure and he was happy for them, but he wanted more, something to life beyond wealth and the stability that supposedly came with it. Friends found him strange, people often thought he was older than he was.

On the express bus to Hpa An, he pondered the unpredictable twists and turns of *kamma,* whether life was predestined or determined afterwards, and how a chance meeting could affect so many emotions – pleasure, sorrow, fury. Deep in thought, at first he didn't notice the passenger next to him nodding wearily again and again. Lin Yaung knew he shouldn't intimidate others by staring, but he couldn't help himself. He suppressed a smile and tried to distract himself by watching the video on the monitor at the front of the bus. It was a comedy, not what he usually enjoyed, so he addressed himself to plans for Hpa An. A friend doing social work had invited him and, busy as he was, he couldn't refuse a friend. Besides, he thought, he could always write about Hpa An, the mountains and people. As a freelancer, he was always on the lookout for ideas for his next article. He figured he'd spend about a week, maybe ten days, in Hpa An, and then return to Yangon and his usual circle of writers, poets, editors and translators.

Lin Yaung fell asleep, waking only when the stranger moved. He ate at the Sein Le Tin rest stop and then fell asleep again. He woke to the voice of a new neighbour, a man wearing black spectacles. "Son, Hpa An is only a short distance from here. Where do you get off?" asked the man, much concerned, for some reason.

"Oh, just tell me when we're near the clocktower. I'll get off there."

"Okay, it's not that far. We're almost there now. See it?"

Lin Yaung looked where the man was pointing, but couldn't make out the landmark in the evening gloom. He took his bag from the overhead rack and shouted down the aisle to the conductor that he'd disembark at the clocktower. The bus pulled to a halt and Lin Yaung bid farewell to the black-spectacled man.

Hints of rain had followed him all the way from Yangon, and now it began to drizzle. Here he was in Hpa An, the town of Mount Zwel Gabin, *Hpa See* drums and *Don Yein* dancing. He dug his friend's address out of his wallet and showed it to a motorbike driver, who assured him he'd get him there.

* * *

Lin Yaung took a deep breath, as was his habit upon arriving in any new town or village. The air was cool and fresh, unlike in Yangon. "Tint Zaw! Hey, Tint Zaw!" he shouted.

Presently, a voice issued from a house and a man emerged. Tint Zaw was in his mid-thirties – the same as Lin Yaung – with fair skin and short hair. On seeing Lin Yaung, he beamed with happiness. "You should've called me, buddy. I'd have come to meet you."

"That's all right, you gave me your address." Lin Yaung looked

Tint Zaw up and down. He hadn't seen him in a while, but nothing had changed.

A few minutes later, there came a smiling woman with pale skin and cropped hair. Tint Zaw introduced her when he saw Lin Yaung staring. "This is my wife, Naw Paw Lu. Isn't she pretty?"

Lin Yaung looked at her again, a little more respectfully. Tint Zaw was right, the Karen woman was very pretty. He silently congratulated his friend on having such a wife.

"Elmu," said Tint Zaw, "this is my good friend Lin Yaung. I met him at the last social work seminar in Yangon and told him he should come visit us sometime. He's a busy man, he earns his living writing."

"Oh, a writer?"

Lin Yaung nodded, but didn't want to say. Sure, he made a living at writing, but how to define what he wrote? "Fiction or non-fiction?" people always asked, "Who publishes you?" He never liked answering those questions. He wanted to write, that's why he wrote. Everything else was unimportant to him.

"Well, are you tired?" asked Tint Zaw. "Take a short rest and shower, we can have dinner later."

Tint Zaw showed him to a room, where he set down his bag, took a shower and changed clothes. He then came out to find dinner already on the table, a wonderful variety of dishes – chicken curry, tomato salad, seaweed salad, soup and fried fish, vegetables with fish paste – and suddenly he realised he was starving.

Over dinner, Lin Yaung replied as best he could to Tint Zaw's questions about his career. Tint Zaw suggested they go into town after dinner. By then the rain had stopped, so Lin Yaung grabbed his camera, which he did wherever he went somewhere new, and they took Tint Zaw's bike. Shwe Hton Maung tea shop was quite small, but apparently had a good cook, so the place was bustling. "Do many tourists come to Hpa An?" he asked Tint Zaw.

"Not so many now, but in time they will."

"True, true."

Over their cups of milk tea, Lin Yaung asked Tint Zaw about his work and home life.

"I'm fine. I have my job, I have an income. And Elmu also

helps me, of course."

"Are your in-laws still alive?"

"Well, her father, U Saw Lan is still alive, but my mother-in-law passed away."

"What does your father-in-law do?"

"He's retired. Used to work with the Karen Literature and Culture Association."

"Really? That's great. I was thinking of writing something about Karen culture while I'm here."

"I'll take you to meet him tomorrow if you want. Well, drink up, my wife's waiting for us."

"Okay, okay," joked Lin Yaung. "I don't want you two to fight because of me."

* * *

U Saw Lan was a stout man with a thick moustache and a strong Karen accent to his spoken Burmese.

"Okay, take a seat," he said to Lin Yaung.

They sat in a living room dominated by a large bookcase neatly stacked with books, magazines and newspapers. A history of the Karen people lay open on the table. Lin Yaung placed his bag on the table and took out a notebook. Tint Zaw explained to U Saw Lan that Lin Yaung was interested in linguistics, and wanted to know the origin of the name 'Hpa An' in particular.

U Saw Lan took a sip of green tea, nodded wisely, and began.

"It's like this. There's a legend, a story about the Dragon Princess and the Frog Prince. They fell in love and the Dragon Princess laid two eggs before she returned to her Dragon Kingdom and he to his domain. The two eggs floated down the Thanlywin River and hatched. One became a frog and the other a dragon. Being different in nature, they fought from the beginning. The Dragon thought his brother looked very tasty and so the Frog hid, by clinging to the side of the mountain, which became known as Hpa Kat Taung, 'Frog Cling Mountain'. But the Dragon was not easily fooled and found where his brother was hiding. So the Frog fled and squeezed into a crack on another mountain, Hpa

Pu Taung, 'Frog Squeeze Mountain'. Again, the Dragon was too clever and the Frog hopped away to yet another mountain, but it was too late. The Dragon caught his brother and ate him. But because they were brothers, the Dragon couldn't stomach the Frog and threw up. The mountain where the Frog fell was forever known as Hpa An Taung, 'Frog Vomit Mountain'."

Lin Yaung scribbled down the story in his notebook as fast as he could.

"Thank you. I was also wondering about Karen youth. You know, marriage rites, things like that."

A smile flickered across U Saw Lan's face as he leaned his back in the chair and took off his glasses. "Hmm, well, according to Karen custom, there's no dowry, but other than that marriage is not so different from in other places. Some villages traditionally favour group marriage, so family members postpone getting married until their siblings do."

While U Saw Lan was talking, in walked a girl. Mid-twenties, shoulder-length hair, short-sleeved blouse – and a nice smile, thought Lin Yaung. "Ko Tint Zaw," she asked, "where's Ama Paw Lu?"

"Oh, Naw Phawl Wah," said Tint Zaw, rising from his chair to introduce her. "This is my wife's sister. She's a Burmese language major at Hpa An University. And this is my friend, Lin Yaung. He's here researching Karen culture for an article."

Her eyes widened in pleasant surprise. "Are you a writer?" she asked with a smile. "I'd love to ask you about it, if you don't mind. I can't pay you, but I could be your guide, take you places you want to go in Hpa An." Lin Yaung liked her from the start.

After the interruption, U Saw Lan went on talking for quite a while, but Naw Phawl Wah stayed until she got a chance to tell Lin Yaung, "Brother, if you're bored, I can show you around town tomorrow."

* * *

Lin Yaung waited for Naw Phawl Wah on the bamboo bench outside Tint Zaw's house. The morning was still and balmy, the sky clear of rain. He checked his bag once again to make sure he had everything – camera, notebook, phone, pen. Before long Naw Phwal Wah arrived with a car and they drove into the town. On the way they passed Kan Thaya, 'Lake Pleasant', with Mount Zwel Gabin mirrored in its waters. The town was quiet, save for a few bikes and *patth na* recitations droning from a temple loudspeaker.

Naw Phwal Wah suggested they first visit a souvenir shop full of Karen red, blue and white fringed waistcoats, t-shirts of Karen heroes and silver jewellery. "See something you like, Brother?" Naw Phwal Wah asked, showing him a beaded purse. "How about this for your girlfriend in Yangon?" she teased.

Lin Yaung just nodded, but didn't buy anything.

"After this we should eat something. There's an excellent restaurant not far from here."

They drove there, and after ordering, Naw Phwal Wah asked, "So what do you write?"

Lin Yaung felt his body tighten as always whenever someone asked this question. He wanted to be regarded as a serious writer who explored important issues, but in actual fact he sold travelogues and the occasional column to make ends meet. He didn't know what to say, but luckily the food arrived to break the uneasy silence. "Well, I write different things, depending on my mood. Sometimes I write poems, the next day it could be a short story."

"Short stories!" Naw Phwal Wah leaned across the table excitely. "Please teach me how to write one. If you don't, I'll tell Ko Tint Zaw," she teased.

Lin Yaung agreed, not because of her silly prod, but because of the passion behind it.

* * *

The following day, Naw Phwal Wah and four of her friends sat in a spare room at Tint Zaw's house, while Lin Yaung explained the different kinds and styles of short stories, point of view, plot and setting. He asked his charges to write a practice paragraph, which they did – really not badly at all. Good, they knew composition, but one day wouldn't be enough, he'd have to teach them for at least a week, which meant staying in Hpa An for a fortnight.

Sigh. He hadn't even told his girlfriend Thel Nu he was going to Hpa An. If he had, she wouldn't have let him go alone. Still, flicking through pictures of her on his mobile phone, he missed her. They'd fought before he left, the usual squabble, she wanting him to get a real job with a regular salary. And the final insult, accusing him of being a dreamer. He sighed again, lost in the images, and didn't notice Naw Phwal Wah standing next to him,

"Brother, we're all going to Zwel Gabin mountain, want to come with us?"

Lin Yaung looked at his watch. It was already 3pm. He was satisfied with the way the day had gone. His students had worked hard, as had he, so why not take a break? Plus he could always write about the mountain when he returned to Yangon. The six of them set out on motorbikes to Zwel Gabin, just ten miles away. The road to the foot of the mountain led through a quiet compound dotted left and right with Buddha statues and ended in a green lake. Naw Phwal Wah and the others snapped selfie after selfie until it started to rain, and they ran under a stone arch for cover – all except for Lin Yaung who stayed by the lake. They called him, warning him he'd get sick, but he refused to move. Naw Phwal Wah figured he was an artist, and artists do as they like. She didn't know the rain was cooling the fire in his heart.

* * *

When Lin Yaung woke, his body was weak and sore. His limbs ached and his feverish head pounded. Not just because of the rain; he'd been thinking too much recently. He found a note from Tint Zaw and his wife saying they'd be away all day at a seminar, when the phone rang. Naw Phwal Wah arrived thirty minutes later.

"Hey, Lin Yaung. You alright? What can I do for you? Should I take you to the clinic?"

Naw Phwal Wah rested her palm on Lin Yaung's forehead. She leaned in close and through the fever he noticed her round eyes.

Naw Phwal Wah saw him staring and blushed. An unexpected gust of wind blew in through the open window and scattered Lin Yaung's notes all over the room. Naw Phwal Wah rushed to collect the papers and found a photograph of a smiling woman with long hair and fair skin. She turned it over. On the back someone had written 'To My Dearest... '

* * *

Lin Yaung continued to teach his students the art of the short story. They'd gained more confidence, asking him questions where once they would have just sat in silence, so in the evenings he browsed the local U Sauk Pan bookshop for sample passages to show them. While Lin Yaung had grown closer to all his students, Naw Phwal Wah had attached herself to him more than the others. What Lin Yaung didn't know was that she'd been observing him closely all week, especially when he'd sit on the bamboo bench after every class and stare off into space. She guessed Lin Yaung's absent moments had to do with the woman in the photograph and wanted to say something, but couldn't bring herself to pry. Still, Lin Yaung *had* kindly given his time to teach, so maybe she could pay him back with a visit to Kan Thaya Lake and, if all went right, tell him what she knew.

* * *

They stopped by a tree at the edge of the lake. The water was clear and still, the silhouette of Mount Zwel Gabin loomed in the distance. It was only 10:30 and the morning breeze had not yet warmed in the morning sun. Naw Phwal Wah kept glancing at Lin Yaung from the corner of her eyes, wondering if she should raise the issue of the woman in the photograph.

"Phwal Wah, did you want to ask me something? About writing?" Lin Yaung asked, aware that she was pretending not to look at him.

"No, you've explained all of that really well. But there *is* something, though I'm not sure I should ask." She hesitated, then spoke up, "Don't be angry with me. I found a photograph of a woman on your table the day you had the fever. May I ask who she is?"

Lin Yaung looked away. Should he tell her the truth? He didn't have to, it was a private matter after all, but Naw Phwal Wah was a friend, and he couldn't lie to her.

"She's my girlfriend. Anything wrong with that?"

"Nothing at all. She's a beautiful lady, only…" Naw Phwal Wah was afraid to push too hard. "You came here without her, and I haven't once seen you call her."

Lin Yaung huffed through his teeth, but Naw Phwal Wah gently put her hand on his arm and asked, "After class, when you sit on the bench, what are you staring at?"

"Umm, it's just that we… we had a fight before I came here." Lin Yaung propped his hand against the tree and related everything that had happened. "She hurt my pride. I was angry, so I just left and came straight here."

Naw Phwal Wah turned away from the reflection of the mountain to face Lin Yaung. "That's a shame. But she must love you, right?"

"Yes, but she doesn't understand why I can't just quit. That's why I am angry with her. She knows me so well, yet she's so different from me."

Naw Phwal Wah sympathised with Lin Yaung who had spent many hours in the class discussing why literature mattered, and the value of stories in exploring and questioning the world. She understood his intent. But as a woman, she also knew the girlfriend hadn't meant to insult him. If anything, she probably adored Lin Yaung and wanted a better life for him than living paycheck to paycheck, writing articles he wasn't even proud of.

"Listen, it seems to me you've jumped to your own conclusions without ever really asking her why she was saying those things. Let me tell you one thing: don't make your writing compete with this girl's love, you can't win. Love has principles too, you know – like understanding each other? When you write, maybe you compare yourself to other writers, but you can't measure a relationship by the standards of others, you can't measure love. Maybe you draw strength from your books, but you can't get angry with her for not understanding that. Literature and love are not the same." Naw Phwal Wah stopped, exhausted.

Lin Yaung looked at her, shocked that this young woman could have such an understanding of life. Her calm words allowed him to think clearly for the first time in ages.

Having caught her breath, Naw Phwal Wah continued. "I know you've heard people say true love never runs smooth, but I don't agree... *and* I can disprove it. For love to last, you need to know how to love. Sure, everyone understands the value of love or why we love, but not *how*. Love that lasts comes from sacrifice and strength. You have to be prepared to make sacrifices and at the same time draw strength from one another. That way, the relationship is built on peace, not conflict, and lets you find meaning in both your lives together. Remember you said the ending of a story can be happy or sad or neither – but doesn't everyone want a happy ending. If you're so stubborn, how will your story end? It had better be happy or I won't be."

Lin Yaung smiled. Naw Phwal Wah was using his own words from only the day before to encourage him. Well, life was like a story with action rising and falling until it reaches a dramatic threshold where only the denouement can follow.

* * *

After a storm come gentle breezes. After darkness, light. After misunderstanding, a clearer vision. Lin Yaung returned to Tint Zaw's house and slept, dreaming of Thel Nu smiling. Naw Phwal Wah was right, lovers shouldn't compete with one another. Early the next morning he asked Tint Zaw to buy him a bus ticket back to Yangon.

Tint Zaw was surprised and wondered why Lin Yaung was so eager to return home.

"Don't worry," Lin Yaung said, "I just have to go back today."

Tint Zaw changed clothes and took Lin Yaung to the bus yard on his motorbike.

"You should stay here a few more days. Next time then, when

you're not in such a rush."

Lin Yaung didn't have time to say goodbye to Naw Phwal Wah, but he silently thanked her for her words the day before. The bus pulled up and Lin Yaung found his seat at the back. He could see the clocktower through the window and for a moment wished he could stay in Hpa An a few more days, as Tint Zaw had suggested, but Thel Nu was waiting.

"Ko Lin Yaung! Ko Lin Yaung!" Someone was calling his name. It was Naw Phwal Wah. Lin Yaung got off the bus, glad to be able to say goodbye. "I can't thank you enough. Because of you, I now understand Thel Nu."

Tint Zaw looked at them both, confused.

Swinging an arm around Tint Zaw's shoulder, Lin Yaung hugged him and said, "I'll explain everything later."

The conductor called out for all passengers to board, the bus was about to leave. Lin Yaung smiled at the brother and sister, got back on and waved goodbye through the open window. As the bus pulled away from the clocktower, he'd already decided to call Thel Nu once he reached Yangon and tell her of Naw Phwal Wah, who made him realise what she meant in his life.

Translated from Burmese by the author

SAW LAMBERT

Saw Lambert (1941 – 2015) was an ethnic Karen educator and writer born in Karen State who served as headmaster of several state schools. As Vice Chairman of the Karen Culture and Literature Association, he oversaw annual summer schools for Karen youth in remote villages. His classes taught the Karen scripts, poetry and history - subjects banned in the government schools at the time - and ensured that the next generation of Karen writing lived on. Saw Lambert passed away two months after the publication of this, his first short story, from which an extract was read at his funeral.

KAW THA WAH THE HUNTER

Originally written in the Sgaw Karen language, 'Kaw Tha Wah the Hunter' deftly imagines a land in flux, where spirits who wander the remote forests clash with the decline of the arrogant colonial dominion and the terrifying advancing new world order. In the protagonist, Kaw Tha Wah, we see the fabled hero drawn from oral legends, who despite untold dangers will ultimately prevail in his journey. Saw Lambert himself lived through three tumultuous political eras, so perhaps it is no wonder that Kaw Tha Wah's quest for happiness and peace mirrors his own people's struggle. While that particular ending has yet to be written, as in all oral histories there is a lesson to be taken from 'Kaw Tha Wah the Hunter', and that is one of hope.

KAW THA WAH
THE HUNTER

ပှၤဟၢးခးအိၣ်တၢ်ဖိကၢ်ၢသးဝး

Like most villages in Karen State, Kappali had a primary school. It was small, just one room with bamboo walls, a thatched roof and a blackboard. Kaw Tha Wah and his sister Naw Thar Mee attended the school every day, as did their friend Naw Mu Htoo.

Once, their teacher Naw Thay asked them, "What do you want to do when you grow up, my dears?"

First, Kaw Tha Wah said he wanted to be a hunter like his father, for then there'd always be good food at home. Naw Thar Mee thought she'd like to be a baker. Of course, she was always thinking about eating. Finally, Naw Mu Htoo dreamed of becoming a weaver, because she liked to wear beautiful dresses. After school the three children would help their parents in the fields, picking vegetables and looking after the pigs and chickens. Everyone in the village was a farmer working the same land, so nobody was richer or poorer than the next family.

As the three children grew, Kaw Tha Wah matured into a handsome young man and Naw Mu Htoo into a beautiful young girl. During the ploughing and harvesting seasons, the whole village would come together in the fields, and Kaw Tha Wah would tease Naw Mu Htoo. It was obvious to the villagers they had fallen for each other, and everyone was pleased. They all liked Kaw Tha Wah. His father taught him the art of hunting as well as farming. Whenever he had free time, Kaw Tha Wah would disappear into the forest around Kappali, and if luck brought him a good catch, he'd share the meat with his neighbours.

One day in the forest, Kaw Tha Wah saw a wild boar and quickly fired his gun. Now Kaw Tha Wah was an excellent shot, but the boar's skin was thick and strong, and the animal ran off into the bush. Kaw Tha Wah followed the bloody tracks deeper into the hills than he'd ever gone before. He saw no village, no paths made by humans, and yet under the thick trees he came upon a wooden hut surrounded by wild boars. Kaw Tha Wah hid behind a tree and watched in surprise as a young girl in a long white Karen dress stepped out of the hut and began to feed the boars. One of them was the boar Kaw Tha Wah had shot. When the young girl saw blood on the boar's back, she cried aloud and rushed into the hut to get medicine. After dressing the boar's wound, the young girl stood up and shouted into the forest.

"Why did you shoot this boar? Shoot whichever boar you like, but never this one again!"

Kaw Tha Wah knew the girl couldn't see him. He just stared at her, captivated by her beauty, not caring about the boar anymore. Then, as if something broke the spell, he suddenly remembered where he was and rushed back home. He didn't go hunting again after that, nor did he tell anyone about his encounter with the strange young girl. Instead, he spent his time cutting and stripping bamboo to weave into baskets.

* * *

This was the time of British rule, and an Englishman was appointed Commissioner for the Karen people. In his travels around the plains and hills, one day he reached the town of Shwe Goun on the banks of the Salween River, only three miles away from Kappali. He heard of Kaw Tha Wah's prowess at hunting and thought to himself, well, if the young man has a gun, he might also be a rebel. So he told his police officers to bring Kaw Tha Wah to Shwe Goun. When Kaw Tha Wah arrived with his village chief, the Englishman took a long look at the gun, then asked the chief about Kaw Tha Wah. The chief replied honestly that Kaw

Tha Wah had a good reputation in the village and everyone liked him. The Englishman decided to test Kaw Tha Wah. "If you really are such a good hunter, then you should be able to shoot. If you hit the target, I will release you."

The Englishman ordered his men to stake a bamboo pole in the middle of the Salween River. The river was wide and the strong currents rocked the bamboo back and forth. The Englishman handed Kaw Tha Wah his English rifle and told him to shoot the bamboo, but Kaw Tha Wah had never used a fancy foreign rifle before and asked if he might use his own homemade gun instead. Word spread around town and soon a crowd gathered on the river bank to watch. Kaw Tha Wah cleaned his gun as best he could and filled it with gunpowder from a small leather bag at his waist. He looked long and hard at the bamboo pole swaying in the river, judged the strength and direction of the wind, then knelt on one knee. The crowd went silent and still. All eyes were on the bamboo pole. Kaw Tha Wah cocked the steel hammer with his thumb, closed one eye, corrected the alignment of the rear and front sights on the barrel, and slowly exhaled. He pulled the trigger and, with a bang, the bamboo splintered into bits. The river bank erupted in cheers and shouts.

The Englishman congratulated Kaw Tha Wah and told him he was free to go. He even presented him with his own rifle as a prize for hitting such a difficult target. On Kaw Tha Wah's return to Kappali, the villagers had already heard of his feat and welcomed him back, especially Naw Mu Htoo.

* * *

British Rule was coming to an end. The war spread even to Karenland, and a Japanese Army contingent was on its way. Naw Mu Htoo's father, a junior officer in the colonial Karen Rifles, was ordered by his British superiors to defend the large town of Hpa Pun, many miles from Kappali. He asked Kaw Tha Wa's father to look after Naw Mu Htoo and her mother while he was away. Only a week after he left, the village chiefs gathered all the villagers to tell them that the Japanese were closing in and could enter the village at any moment.

Naw Mu Htoo's house was at the edge of the village, and Kaw Tha Wah knew the Japanese would search it first. So he went to Naw Mu Htoo to ask her and her mother to move in with his father for protection, while he and a friend, Pha Kha Lay Phoe, would guard their house. Pha Kha Lay Phoe slept early, but Kaw Tha Wah tossed and turned for hours, restlessly thinking behind his closed eyes of Naw Mu Htoo and their uncertain fate.

Kaw Tha Wah was awoken by a loud rustling, to find two Japanese soldiers standing over him, the bayonets on their rifles gleaming even in the dark. Behind them stood an officer holding a coil of rope. Where was Pha Kha Lay Phoe? Had he escaped or been tied up outside? As the two soldiers lifted Kaw Tha Wah to his feet, a noise in the forest distracted them, and Kaw Tha Wah saw his chance. He hit one soldier and shoved the other to the floor and ran away. All the houses in the village were deserted. It wasn't until morning that he found his family and Naw Mu Htoo hiding in the forest. They told him what had happened the night before. Pha Kha Lay Phoe had seen the Japanese soldiers enter the house where Kaw Tha Wah was sleeping and, assuming he'd been captured, ran to warn the other villagers. Just then, two men arrived with word that the Japanese were advancing quickly. It wasn't safe for Naw Mu Htoo and her mother to stay there any longer, so the men were to escort them both to the village of Htee Ka Haw far below the Dawna Mountains, where the chief Hpa Pa Law, who was related to Kaw Tha Wah's mother, promised to keep them safe.

The Japanese were still in the village, but Kaw Tha Wah couldn't let Naw Mu Htoo leave without the basket he'd woven especially for her. He crept back into the village and grabbed the basket without being seen. He'd been meaning to give it to her later, but now this might be his last opportunity.

"Little sister Mu Htoo," he said, handing her the basket, "whenever you use this basket, think of me."

"Brother Kaw Tha Wah, how could I forget you? Here, to help you remember me too." Naw Mu Htoo reached into a bag and pulled out a headscarf she had woven herself. She promised Kaw

Tha Wah she'd follow the Karen tradition of raising a pig until he came back to her. Kaw Tha Wah smiled and swore she'd see him again before long.

For the next couple of years, the villagers of Kappali lived in the forest, but the Japanese never stopped hunting them. One by one, they were all captured, including Kaw Tha Wah and his family. The soldiers dug a big pit in the centre of the village and threatened they'd all be buried there. The villagers, both Christian and Buddhist, prayed together, until a plane overhead dropped a flutter of leaflets telling the Japanese to surrender to the nearest British Army camp. Atomic bombs had devastated cities in Japan. The war was over. The soldiers fled into the forest, and the villagers celebrated their freedom with singing and dancing.

* * *

The war destroyed most of Kappali, and many houses had to be rebuilt. Fields that lay fallow for many harvests had to be re-ploughed. Kaw Tha Wah and his sister, Naw Tha Mee, worked hard with the other villagers, and by year-end they had a good rice yield and a full store of fish. After the harvest, Kaw Tha Wah asked his parents for permission to see Naw Mu Htoo and they prayed for his safe journey, for the mountain path to Htee Ka Haw was rough. But Karenland was now at peace, and Kaw Tha Wah's steps were happy and quick, knowing he'd soon be meeting Naw Mu Htoo again. Sleeping in ruined huts along the way, it took him four days to cross the mountains. Though he saw many animals, he didn't hunt, eating instead the food his sister had prepared. Once he got to Htee Ka Haw, he went to see Naw Mu Htoo's mother and father to tell them he'd come with his parents' blessings. They welcomed him, for they knew how sad their daughter had been to leave him behind. Kaw Tha Wah rested, took a quick shower and a meal, then Naw Mu Htoo's father went to sit in the shade to cut bamboo strips while her mother dug roots and sprouts from the garden.

Alone in the house, Kaw Tha Wah drew close to Naw Mu Htoo and said, "Sister Mu Htoo, wherever I was, I always thought of you. I came for you just like I promised."

"Are you sure? I thought you had forgotten me. I always put your bamboo basket next to my bed when I sleep."

"I believe you. I also carry your scarf with me every day."

They talked for a while longer, until Kaw Tha Wah couldn't wait any longer and asked Naw Mu Htoo to marry him.

"But the pig is still small," she said.

"Don't worry about the pig. It's not important."

Naw Mu Htoo's parents had no objection, for they loved Kaw Tha Wah as a son. As his father was across the mountains, Kaw Tha Wah asked his uncle Hpa Pa Law to request Naw Mu Htoo's hand in marriage in their stead in accordance with Karen custom. All approved and they celebrated with a cooked chicken.

* * *

Kaw Tha Wah's parents crossed the mountains for the wedding. The preparations took two days, and the ceremony was held before the whole village on the third day. The day before his parents returned to Kappali, Kaw Tha Wah decided it was time he started hunting again. With permission from his uncle, he set off into the Dawna Mountains, but however far he walked the forest was barren of wildlife. Tired, he rested under a large tree, examining the sights and barrel of his rifle, when he noticed an old man walking towards him.

"My grandson," rasped the old man, "could you give me a puff on your cheroot?"

Kaw Tha Wah's uncle had warned him how evil spirits guarded the lands around. "Grandpa, if you want to smoke, then open your mouth."

The old man yawned. Kaw Tha Wah aimed the gun and fired.

"Grandson, your cheroot is so mild," was all the old man said.

"Then just wait a bit, I'll give you a stronger cheroot."

Kaw Tha Wah poured more gunpowder and a heavier lead ball into the rifle.

"Grandpa, open your mouth again."

This time Kaw Tha Wah quickly thrust the barrel of the gun

deep inside the old man's open mouth and pulled the trigger. The old man vanished in a swirl of smoke, and Kaw Tha Wah thought to himself, now the forest is mine.

From then on, whenever Kaw Tha Wah, Chief Hpa Pa Law and his friends went hunting in the forest, they heard birds singing in the trees and animals running in the bush. They only shot what boar or deer they needed and when the sun set behind the village, Naw Mu Htoo and her neighbours would cook for everyone. As they ate and drank and talked and sang together, Kaw Tha Wah thought to himself that only friends and relations united in love for one other could find real happiness.

*Translated from Sgaw Karen to Burmese by the author,
and from Burmese to English by Khin Hnit Thit Oo*

MALI HKU SHINI

Mali Hku Shini (b.1988) is an ethnic Kachin born in Sumdu Ga (Nbu Baw) village, Ma Chang Baw Township in Kachin State. He learnt Ka-hprek, a traditional Kachin martial-arts form while a teenager and trains the next generation from his gym in the Manau Cultural ground in Myitkyina, the capital of Kachin State. He is assistant treasurer of the Kachin Culture and Literature Co-operation, an association that strives to preserve and develop Kachin cultural forms such as literature, language, music, traditional knowledge and textiles. He writes health and sports related articles in the Jinghpaw language for the *Kachin Times* journal.

A BRIDGE MADE FROM CORD

The mining town of Hpakant is the source of the purest jade in the world. For centuries this jade has been coveted, first by the Chinese emperors, then by the British and now soldiers from both sides of the conflict that has erupted once more in Kachin State. In his semi-autobiographical story, Mali Hku Shini invokes a nightmarish vision of loss and suffering. Landscapes are ravaged, men and women are discarded like the rocks they scrabble for. The protagonist, Zaw Htwae, is a visitor to this hellish town, but the hope he brings with him is too little to counteract the anger and despair that ripples intensely through the narrative. 'A Bridge Made from Cord', originally written in the Jinghpaw language, is a solemn warning to all those who seek profit from blood and jewels.

A BRIDGE MADE FROM CORD

Mahkrai Hkrai Noi

The fog comes early in the morning. A person or two passes me on the otherwise empty street. As I exhale, an early winter breeze carried my breath away like smoke to unclear places in the distance. I shiver. I feel so cold without my thick coat. I walk to a small bank under a bridge suspended by rope, and stare at the thin water in Uru Creek, stained with sweetened-tea-coloured mud.

"Where has your beauty gone?" I wonder out loud, for I had heard from Kachin songs from old days of how beautiful the land here was, with wild birds flying in green hills and valleys, and fish swimming in crystal-clear water. Now, I can't find any of these things, the land I see has changed. Has it been destroyed by mankind, or sacrificed for us? Or is it our fault, our Kachin people's, for not being able to protect our lands? I can't find the answer, but I do know that once our ancestors guarded the Uru region well and now it has fallen into different hands, the hands of companies and corporations.

I walk up to the bridge and stand at its centre. Looking at the barren, collapsed hills around me, I ask the Uru Creek below another question. "Is there a difference between those hills and my life?' But it doesn't answer me. So I ask the bridge instead, 'Do you recall a story that started from here, from this very place?" It too has no reply, but as the current of the Uru Creek takes its muddy waters onwards I grip the handrail of the bridge and my mind stumbles to the past.

* * *

Ten years ago I went to Hpa Kant in the west of Kachin State. Most people come to this town dreaming of being a *Law Pan,* but I was there for another reason, to teach *Kahprek.* Most Kachin people know of Master U La Zein La Htwae, who invented this martial art as a way for the Kachin to defend themselves. I taught it in the hope it would free my people from the slavery of drugs. I held my courses mornings and evenings on the ground floor of a Baptist church in Ngapyawtaw Township. It was called the Jade Church, because several of its brick walls were decorated with Hpa Kant's famous deep green jade cuttings.

Life in Hpa Kant wasn't easy at first and I became ill. I went to the pharmacy and bought three doses of four different medicines, which cost me 3,000 kyats. I still had 5,000 kyats in hand, so I spent another 900 on three rehydration salt packets. It helped me to feel better, but it wasn't the welcome I was looking for in Hpa Kant. In time, however, I became friendly with one of my trainees. Robert was a short boy, brown skin, a little fat, always laughing, always talking. Whenever he was with his friends, he'd proudly introduce me to them. "This is my Kahprek trainer, Master Zaw Htwae from Myitkyina."

One day, I went to the local KBZ bank with Robert and, thanks to him, I was introduced to one of the bank-tellers, Ah Nang. I'm not the kind of man to fall for a girl just because of her beauty, but I did notice that she was a girl who didn't wear *thanakha* well. On the way back from the bank, Robert was chattering, "If you look carefully, you'll see she's actually quite beautiful. She's my friend, I know her well. She's educated, good at cooking and housekeeping and everything." The second time I saw Ah Nang was at the Jade Church, when she read a passage from the Bible during a Hpa Kant Regional Christian Youth meeting. While reading on stage, she looked frequently at me, so I smiled and she smiled back.

I began to see her more often after that. Twice a day, in fact, every morning and evening, from opposite sides of the same busy street that we both walked, she on her way to the bank in the morning, me on my way back from training; she on the way back from the bank in the evening, me on my way to training. Despite the thirty feet of road between us, we started to build a bridge of our own. It was small at first, just smiles and glances, but over time the bridge drew us closer and I could hear her whisper, "Are you going back?" and I'd reply, 'Yes, take care." My pupils Robert and Pan Aung began to notice the bridge and even mocked it, saying, "Around here, you got to walk quickly." I didn't mind.

* * *

Most afternoons, I was free, so one day I decided to go and look for *ye-ma-sei*, unwashed stones. It was only after I came to Hpa Kant that I learned about the raw, low-quality jade thrown away by the big companies. Pan Aung lived near my place, so he offered to come with me, "You're not far from Hmaw Maung La Yan. I pick ye-ma-sei over there, too."

I slipped on a pair of long socks, doubled over to protect my feet, and a pair of strong shoes, then stuffed a raincoat and diamond hammer in my backpack. Pan Aung smiled at me and said, "Master, now you look like a real prospector."

"Oh yeah? Hope that means I find a good piece of jade."

He looked me up and down one last time and asked, "Did you pack water, Master? You should take something to eat as well."

On the way, Pan Aung told me about the old days, when prospectors would use iron poles, picks and shovels to extract the stones. By now, however, Hmaw Maung La Yan had been taken over by companies who fenced off their own hills' compounds with iron roofs, employee hostels, fuel tanks and machines. Huge machines. A big company might own up to forty bulldozers and another sixty trucks to haul away soil. "They can clear a whole mountain in less than six months," said Pan Aung, slicing his hand along the horizon, cutting it away. Hundreds of these companies work in Hpa Kant, and when they finish with the earth they dig up, they just dump it. "That's where we look," Pan Aung continued. "If you find a good piece of jade in those piles of mine residue, you need to sneak away quietly. If people from the company found out, they'd want it back it."

Now that I saw it with my own eyes, I felt miserable. Watching the locals claw their way through the dumped soil, it was no better than when the farmers in my village fed rice to their chickens. Hens, roosters and chicks of all different shapes and sizes rush in, screech and fight. We Kachins are like animals caged up by foreign companies. I myself turned chicken that day, scratching the ground to find something, anything.

* * *

The sun was hot. Sitting on the pile of residue, taking a rest, drinking water and gazing from afar at our fellow prospectors, Pan Aung flicked a stone away and said, "You know, some companies don't even let us pick the unwashed stones. They guard them with men and guns. And you know something else? They grade the companies here depending on the number of machines they use. The largest is A, then B and the smallest C."

"And how many of those are owned by Kachins?" I asked.

"Some, but less than you can count on ten fingers all told. Plus, they're all are only C grade, the smallest." Pan Aung thought for a second, then added, "Well, maybe U Ywup Zaw Khaung's company is B grade. Probably used to be A, but well, others steal our people's land, so..." Pan Aung's voice trailed off.

Spending the whole day at the mine was tiring, but I was lucky that day. I didn't find a stone worth thousands, but I did find something worth much more: Ah Nang on the little suspension bridge connecting Hpa Kant to Mashi Ka Htaung. We often met here to talk, leaning over the handrail together to greet the sunset. As the weeks passed, I wanted to tell her how I felt, but I held back the words, wary of what she might say, afraid I'd ruin what we already had. But that wasn't enough for me. I didn't plan it, or think it through, but eventually one evening, as we stood together on the bridge, I held her hand and told her. She blushed and lowered her head to her chest. I waited, sick, for what she would say in return. After a long while, she sighed, "I knew you'd say this one day," but then added, "It's impossible, Zaw Htwae."

"Why? Can you tell me?" I asked. My voice trembled. I felt helpless. She didn't answer. "Please, let me know, why?" I pleaded.

She looked away, then back at me, as if she wanted to say something but thought better of it. "No, it's nothing," she said finally.

* * *

I didn't see Ah Nang for a while after that night. I spent my days alone, depressed, until a pupil of mine, Zaw San, asked if I wanted to pick stones at Hmaw Lon Khin. I needed the distraction, so we set out that very day on a Chinese 125cc motorbike. After only a few miles, Zaw San slowed down.

"Are we there already?" I asked, leaning on Zaw San.

"No, Master, but I wanted to show you something. Look down there."

He pointed towards a row of bushes by the side of the road below. A steady stream of Chinese motorbikes rode in and out kicking up clouds of dust. Old men and young boys squatted alone as if they were peeing, others sat face to face as if in deep conversation. Still others queued in a crooked line toward a hut roofed with a blue tarp.

"That's where they sell opium, Master," said Zaw San, answering my unasked question.

I was shocked. "What? Really!"

"Over there, that blue hut, that's where they sell it."

I peered at the small opium market. All I could say was, "What a terrible place!"

Zaw San replied, knowing the scene was common in Hpa Kant. "Well, all the jade mines are like this." Maybe for Zaw San and others who lived here it meant nothing, but for nearly a week the image of my people queuing up for heroin I couldn't shake.

* * *

Staying in Hpa Kant, I came to know its stories well. I hadn't known anything about jade before. I thought all dark lava-coloured stones were jade, although I'd heard that jade is heavier than normal stones. I then learned that when a stone looks like jade and feels heavy, you should crack it open with a diamond-headed hammer. Prospectors more knowledgeable than I would come to offer their insights. They told me that once you split the stone, you should spit on it and wipe off the dirt to see its quality. Others would take the piece from my hand and lick it, even after I spat on it, just to make sure. They taught me about the different grades of jade, their quality, purity and colour. They showed me how to avoid being crushed to death when a truck poured unwanted soil down the hillside. Dirt, rocks and stones would tumble down to the waiting ants, who'd scramble for first pickings, often dislodging a boulder that would roll, crashing down onto the slower ants below. If you're an ant at the top, you need to call out, 'Stone!' as loud as you can. If not, the other ants will curse you and sometimes beat you. The word has saved many lives in Hpa Kant. This is what it means to be Kachin and dream of a different tomorrow: a jade bridge crossing over from poverty to a life free from it. I too became a *ye-ma-sei thama*, a prospector of unwashed stones. We all found lots of stones, but almost none of them were jade.

* * *

It had been a long time since I'd seen Ah Nang. We never met across the road in the mornings and evenings, unlike before. I guess she walked a different way to and from work. Just before I left Hpa Kant to return to my studies in Myitkyina, I bumped into Htwae Seng, a friend of Ah Nang, and immediately asked him about her.

"She does like you," he said, "you should know that, but she isn't sure about you yet. She worries what people will think if she is seen with you, especially now, with all the rumours of her father." He paused. "This is a secret, okay? If Ah Nang knew I was telling you this, she'd be very angry with me. Her father is a Baptist preacher. Apparently, he left the family for another woman, so everyone's watching them a little too closely right now."

* * *

I completed another year of my degree studies at Myitkyina University and came back to Hpa Kant as soon as I could. I asked Htwae Seng to inform Ah Nang of my return, as I wanted to believe she still might feel something for me, but Ah Nang never visited me at the Jade Church. A friend, a girl from my home town came to visit, and Ah Nang saw us walking together. I smiled at Ah Nang, from across our usual street, but her face was clouded in doubt. I couldn't blame her. When I saw her a week later with another boy, my face too darkened. Many friends knew about my feelings for her. One of them named Zaw Hseng attended her church. One evening, we went to Seit Nyein teahouse, and he asked me, "What do you really know about her?"

I didn't know what to say.

"I want to tell you, as a friend, you should forget her," Zaw Hseng continued.

"Why?"

He took another sip of his tea and considered what to say. "When she was young, she contracted malaria. It changed her, made her a little crazy. I guess she's better now, but…"

Why should I write off a girl just because of that? "Let's go," I said, draining my cup.

Slowly, I rekindled my friendship with Ah Nang. We began to smile at each other from across the street, re-tying the threads that had snapped. On the rope bridge across Uru Creek, I held her hand once more and promised to love her, but all she'd say was, "No, *Sra* Zaw Htwae, it's impossible between you and me."

At midnight on the verandah of my hostel, I played guitar and sang the Kachin ballad 'My love, my heart tells me it can't live without you' to the light of her little house that was always on in the valley opposite. Weeks passed, and soon I had to return to Myitkyina for my final exams. Ah Nang looked at me for a while, then asked, "When will you be back?"

I'd made up my mind never to return, but instead I lied, "I don't know yet!"

I caught a Hi-Lux pickup out of Hpa Kant along a road that crisscrossed the high mountain ridges – a single lane so narrow that cars could only go one way, and should one of these cars break down, you'd be stuck there for days. In summer, dust from the lorries made it difficult to breathe, and in the rainy season, elephants had to pull cars stuck in the mud. This was the main road from the jade mines to Myitkyina, the capital of Kachin State, where I sat for my exams.

After my exams, some friends and I were asked to help with security for that year's *Manau* Festival. The field on the bank of the Irrawaddy was mown and swept clean. The wealthy U Yup Zaw Khawn and Festival Committee members in their traditional Lai *longyi*, Lai turbans and black jackets walked around the shops, *pandals* (stages) and thatch-roofed committee huts. Little by little, the Manau field swelled with thousands of people from all the different Kachin groups in silver-gong decorated costumes, silver swords and colourful turbans. The pastor finished the opening prayers and then came the *Naung Shaung,* the Manau dance leading troop, wearing turbans made from bird feathers, peacock tails and wild boar's horn. Behind the Naung Shaungs, came the important leaders of the noble tribes, then the men and women from their villages. The first, sweet, notes of the traditional flute came, followed by the deeper tones of the buffalo horn with the rumbling of drums and crash of the cymbals. 'Tong... tong...tong... aay... Oh Lord in the highest of heaven... Oh the creator of all mankind... aay... aww lay lay... woo... tong... tong... tong...! Whenever we hear that song, that rhythmic call of the Manau, every Kachin heart shivers as the blood of our ancestors before us flows again.

In the old days, only noble *Duwas* could celebrate the Manau dance. Behind their long house, they'd clear a field and erect wooden Manau posts, where royal relatives and villagers would sit and drink and eat and dance and tell stories for nine days. The guests would bring presents, such as a buffalo, a much prized animal, gifts which would have to be reciprocated when the recipients, in turn, held their own *Manau*. This is why only the Duwas used to hold a Manau: they were the only ones who owned the land and slaves to afford it. Things are different now. The Duwas have gone, or at least their powers have, and within the framework of Christianity, the Manau Festival is organized by a committee of elders and sponsored by rich men.

* * *

After the Manau Festival, I returned one last time to Hpa Kant. I didn't try to contact Ah Nang. It was clear to me that our story would not end well. Even after Htwae Seng told me Ah Nang did nothing but talk about me and wanted to meet me, I distanced myself from her. I did my last training sessions at the Jade Church, and left Hpa Kant and Ah Nang behind.

* * *

It was two years since I left Hpa Kant and let myself forget Ah Nang. Sometimes, I'd meet boys from that frontier jade town and be reminded of her. I might mention her name, hoping perhaps that they knew her, but soon I stopped doing even that.

I met Htwae Hseng again, and he passed me Ah Nang's number, saying, "She's waiting for you to come ask for her hand." I was curious, I admit, to hear her voice, to hear if she would say those words and if she was indeed waiting for me. So I tried to call her that evening, and every evening for the next four days, but the line just didn't connect. And once again, I soon forgot about her.

Then, one day, while I was playing billiards, Zaw Hseng came up to me.

"How are you, Master? It's been a long time."

"I'm fine, Zaw Hseng. How about you? What do you do now? Are you still picking jade stones?"

"Well, that's all we can do in Hpa Kant!"

"Did you find any big stones?"

We chatted for a while before he asked me, "Did you hear about Ah Nang?"

"No, why?"

"She died."

He spoke so bluntly, I was sure he was joking.

He wasn't: "No, I'm not. Why would I joke about something like this?"

I stared at him blankly for I don't know how long. I was shocked, I didn't know what to say.

"How?" I breathed, as my heart began to weep.

"She died of heart disease. She fainted in Hpa Kant, so we brought her to Myitkyina. Her body is in the local mortuary."

I went to her funeral at Jaw Bum cemetery, laid a rose on her casket, then helped cover it with soil. Htwae Hseng was with me, almost in tears.

"Here, this is Ah Nang's diary. I'm sorry, I read it. She wrote how much she wanted to be with you."

I knew then I had been wrong: I should have seen her that one last time in Hpa Kant, I should have tried harder to call.

"Everything is my fault. I'm sorry, Ah Nang." With these words, I said my farewell.

* * *

You little bridge of Uru Creek, you are still here, though the thread between Ah Nang and myself has been cut, like the disappearing mountains of the Uru Region and time and tide themselves, never to return.

Translated from Jinghpaw to Burmese by the author,
and from Burmese to English by Khin Hnit Thit Oo

KHIN PANN HNIN

Khin Pann Hnin (d. 2017) was a writer, doctor and journalist born in the delta town of Myaung Mya, Ayeyarwaddy Division. She is the author of two short story collections, *The Walkers* and *Age Poem and Other Stories*, as well as two novels *The Far End of the Clouds* and *Dreams of a Heartbeat Garden*. A story, *Zero Degrees Centigrade,* was translated into Japanese by the Daido Foundation. Her most recent work was a chapbook of romance poems published by Seikku Cho Cho in 2015. She passed away in Mandalay in 2017.

A PLEDGE OF LOVE
TO THE MALIKHA RIVER

The mighty Ayeyarwaddy River cuts Myanmar in two but starts life at the merging of two tributary sisters, the Malikha and N'mai Kha. In this haunting tale of regret and nostalgia, Khin Pann Hnin constructs her narrative around layers of memories anchored in the landscape. As an era of missed opportunities confronts Sayama Thinn upon her return to the source of the Ayeyarwaddy, and we are drawn into a shifting world of time and place where one decision can force everlasting and fatal consequences. 'A Pledge of Love to the Malikha River' unfolds in several locations: the Delta region of lower Myanmar, far away Kachin State and Lashio, the same embattled northern Shan State town that Khin Pann Hnin herself worked in as a government doctor before being dismissed for treating student victims of the 1988 revolution.

A PLEDGE OF LOVE
TO THE MALIKHA RIVER

မလိခမြစ်ရဲ့ သစ္စာတိုင်တေးတစ်ပုဒ်

From the cabin window, I see small clouds floating across the sky – some dense and silvery, barely moving, some in clusters or layers; others white and light grey; most lined with golden sunlight. Catching the wisps, the memories of clouds moving quickly towards the horizon, my heart leaps up all of a sudden. I was surprised my heartbeats were still fresh. Could it be because I was going to the land of the Kachin again?

I generally think of myself as hardened and thick-skinned. All my life, that which I have seen and witnessed I assumed had left me empty of feelings and emotions – and yet it seems I was wrong. Right after taking off from Mandalay Airport, still far from Myitkyina, those clouds made me frightened. Not because I was flying so high; rather, it was the memories of a place special to me: the Myitsone, the confluence of the Malikha and Maykha tributaries that is the birthplace of the Ayeyarwaddy River.

I can picture the rock outcroppings, the wide sandbar where the waters meet. On those two riverbanks where the Ayeyarwaddy begins, pebble pools will be waiting in silence. Would that our steps from years before had left lasting imprints on the banks!

As the plane nears Myitkyina, the Ayeyarwaddy with her wide sandbanks comes into view. And over there, that must be Karein Naw, where the mountains and river meet at the bridge. The plane descends, the stewardess instructs us to fasten our seatbelts, then an excitement surges over me as we gently touch down on the tarmac.

Myitkyina Airport hasn't changed much, save for a couple of new buildings under construction. In the pale yellow sunlight, so precious in cold weather, I'm delighted to see old friends waiting for me as I leave the airport.

"Hey, Mong Ban! Thu Raw! Kachin Thet Mon Myint! Kaung Mei!" I call out their names one by one. Ja Sai Noai has always been our 'Kachin Thet Mon Myint' because she's as beautiful as the popular actress. Kaung Mei Mai is still single and remarkably composed. Mong Ban hasn't lost her athletic figure. And Thu Raw seems wholly unchanged, reserved beyond her years.

"Sayama!" They rush towards me shouting, "You look as young as when you were last here."

"Don't say that! Sayama is more beautiful than ever . . ." They can't wait their turn and speak over each other. All except for Kaung Mei Mai, who just smiles as usual. Being with my girls, I know I'm finally walking among the Manau poles again.

* * *

"Footsteps may leave their mark in the sand, only to vanish before long. Those rocks, however, will last forever, Thinn. We can imagine the age of those rocks from their touch. The love I feel for you is the same as them, everlasting. It's impossible that you cannot feel my love for you, Thinn. Someday you will."

It's been years since he gazed softly into my eyes and spoke those words.

Most people are only interested in the clear waters of the two tributaries and the stones that bring good luck. Yet he compared his love for me to the everlasting rocks. I was afraid. I'd forgotten he was an intelligent man, but also a serious one. My mind drifted like the rivers. At that time, his words hit their intended targets, right at the centre: my affection for him.

"It's a good thing girls are not easily convinced, but why don't you trust anyone, especially me?" He paused a moment and repeated, "Why don't you trust me?"

It wasn't because I didn't trust him. I just didn't want to be unfaithful to someone else. In fact, although my work took me to Myitkyina, I'd come to the Myitsone to give him the answer he wanted to hear, that I would love him in return. But the rocks protested my decision, making me tremble inside. A sad face suddenly appeared, pleading with me not to give him my love.

… Ma Thinn, can't you wait any longer?
Ma Thinn, can't you wait any longer for Tun?
Ma Thinn, can't you wait… ?

… The words reminded me of something, of someone else. Out of the rocks in the Malikha, Tun was watching me helplessly.

Tun was a childhood classmate of mine. We passed our exams together in the Ayeyarwaddy Delta market town of Myaungmya and both attended Yangon University. We were very close. He became involved in student protests, while I concentrated on my medical studies. After the 1962 revolution and subsequent unrest, he went into exile in a 'liberated area', saying he'd be leaving for a while – a very long 'while'. I didn't hear a thing after that until I came across an interview with a 'freedom fighter' named Bo Thinn Tun from the wilds of the Thai border. It broke my heart. The boy I'd known as Tun Thiha Kyaw had adopted my name 'Thinn' for his *nom de guerre.*

This was a time when anyone could be taken away for questioning, and my parents were worried that eventually they'd come for me. Yet however grave their concerns, I somehow reassured them with a calmness even I didn't believe. There'd been no further contact between us, and I never heard the name 'Bo Thinn Tun' again. Though as long as there were people fighting for the people of Myanmar, I knew he'd be with them. I believed that more than anything.

It was long after Tun left my life that U Ko Ko Kyaw – or 'Ko' for short – confessed his love for me. We'd been working in the same department for a long time and knew each other quite well. My parents were favourably impressed. He acted like a gentleman, and when he proposed, they pressed me to accept – at least my mother did. My father said it was up to me to decide. I once overheard my mother scold my father, "You know nothing!

She's still waiting for... that rebel." To which my father replied, "If that's what she wants, no one can stop her."

So I told my mother, "Don't worry, I wouldn't marry Tun unless he returns legally or there's peace in our country."

"I doubt he'll return," she scoffed. "And as for peace, that will take a long time. You just listen to me. Whose life are you trying to save with this dream? You need to think about yourself."

Of course, she was right. I was an only child. I couldn't be like other women and drop everything just because I was in love. I had to consider my parents' feelings, I told myself. Then suddenly one night, I had a dream where Tun said goodbye and walked further and further away until I couldn't see him anymore.

* * *

"We have some questions for you, please come with us." It was a woman's voice.

What was so important that she had to bang so loudly on my door this late at night? This was in Lashio, near the Chinese border, where I'd been employed as part of a contagious diseases control programme. Looking down from my window I saw a policewoman in uniform. When I opened the front door, a man in an Army officer's uniform walked in uninvited.

"You're going to have to come with us. We have some questions for you."

Confused and scared, as if awake in a nightmare, I was taken to the town hall, where I saw a man from my same department. My fear reflected on his face as well.

"Why did they bring you here, Sayama?" he asked in surprise, then lowered his voice to a whisper: "My younger brother is an underground activist, but you... ?"

That very night I was taken to the 'safe' state-run Shweli Guesthouse. They offered me coffee and ordered me to sleep in the room. What worried me most, however, was who might know I'd been called in for questioning. Lashio was a small town, and it wouldn't take much for rumours to spread. If they did, my career was finished.

I figured it had something to do with Tun. The last time I went home, my mother had been worried. She'd even reminded me, "Don't contact that rebel", though in actual fact I wouldn't have known how. After years of no contact, what could I possibly have to say to interrogators?

The following morning, a policeman and an elderly woman came to take me to the 'Artillery Guesthouse' for breakfast. They showed me to a large, clean-swept room – a dining hall? – where I was left alone at a table set with coffee, biscuits and fruit. I ate and ate until I was full because I didn't know what would happen next. In those days, the feared Military Intelligence would still suspect you even if you hadn't done anything wrong. All of a sudden, I thought of my parents. They would be distressed if they knew. My mother would wail, "Didn't I tell you that rebel of yours would bring you trouble one day?"

At about nine o'clock, a young military officer came. "Before we get started, Sayama, I've got something to tell you," he said, opening a folder he carried under his arm to lay out various papers. "I just want to know about you and Boh Thinn Tun." The exact question I'd expected.

The officer handed me a photograph. It was easy to identify his face in the bust portrait, though he looked much older than his years. He was wearing what my mother scorned as a rebel uniform. I didn't want to use the term 'rebel' for Tun. He just fought for what he believed in. At that moment, I suddenly remembered my mother's words "What else can those rebels do to survive besides exhort money?" I shouted back, "You know nothing, Mother. Nowadays men like Tun live on dollars provided by foreign organizations."

"If your rebel lives on foreign dollars, that just shows how little faith he has in what he is supposedly fighting for," my mother continued.

I didn't want to argue any more. I knew better than anyone how resolute his faith was. Had he really become a lieutenant in his organisation? I couldn't help but smile.

"Happy to see your childhood sweetheart, are you, Sayama?" The officer's voice shook me from my fond reverie.

"Well, yes, I haven't seen him since he left," I said.

"And you didn't stop him from leaving?"

"Honestly, I don't know how to answer your question. Yes, I did try to persuade him not to go. But at the same time, I also thought it was better to let him be who he wanted to be."

A grimace hardened the officer's face. "I'm sorry, Sayama. Bo Thinn Tun was killed last month." He explained very graphically how Tun was shot in a battle, to convince me Bo Thinn Tun was really dead. I didn't want to picture it, though I suppose between all the guns and bombs death was his daily life. He'd been shot by a Burmese soldier, but at that moment I preferred to think it a sacrifice for something he believed in.

"Would you like to see a photo of the body?" asked the officer. "It doesn't matter either way."

"Yes, please. And if possible, I'd like to keep it."

"You can look, but we can't give it to you," he duly informed me.

I'll never forget how Tun lay twisted on the ground. "Please be my same Tun in your next life," I whispered to myself, holding the image of his corpse.

The officer was watching me. I just smiled back.

"You're very strong, Sayama," he said to me.

"I'm not one to burst into tears," I replied. "I'll grieve for him in my own way. He lost his life believing in something."

"I won't criticise your opinions, but we called you here because among his seized possessions was a diary with entries about you. Also a photograph of you."

I reached for the diary. The photo showed a girl in pigtails by a staircase at our high school.

The officer continued, "Sayama, we'll send you back home this evening. We're very sorry to have brought you here like this, but it would have been illegal had we just come to your house and given you these things."

"Thank you very much. I will remember your kindness."

The Artillery's Guesthouse was directly in front of Lashio's famous Elephant Hill, so called because of the resemblance to a crouching behemoth – body, forehead, trunk, tail. At the foot of

Elephant Hill were several smaller 'knuckle' hills of green, red and yellow trees. There was a sentry box not far away. The entrance to the guesthouse was to the side, not in front, where an armed soldier stood guard. Was he there on regular duty or just to keep his eyes on me? I stared at the hills late into the night, until the elephant finally retreated under the shadows and I remembered to go to bed. I'd been told they would send me home that evening, but they lied. I didn't know what to expect next. Everything was in their hands – they had absolute control.

The next morning, I was escorted from the guesthouse back to my house. On the way home, I could no longer choke back my emotions. My colleagues who had been waiting anxiously for me were worried to see the tears streaming down my cheeks.

"Don't worry, it's nothing. I'll tell you all about it later. Right now, I just want to rest."

Not long after that I resigned from my job. Not just because I couldn't stand the accusing eyes all around me or Military Intelligence having questioned me about my rebel childhood sweetheart. I was more hurt that my colleagues still doubted me even after I'd told the truth. And to be perfectly honest, I couldn't stay in the same office anymore with Ko Ko Kyaw, whom I'd once thought a man of principle but now was obviously avoiding me. Even worse, he was spreading rumours the reason I'd been interrogated because I was 'intimate' with Tun.

Very well, I had to abandon my job, my position, my income and also a man who had once claimed he loved me. I wasn't upset at all. I'd left because of Tun, who thought of me until the day he died. How stupid of me to even consider returning Ko Ko Kyaw's love! True, I almost caved in, but thankfully those everlasting Malikha rocks had taught me how to be firm.

Having quit my job in Lashio, I returned to Yangon, where I became depressed doing nothing all day. Then one day, I was invited by a European NGO to work with Myanmar ethnic groups. Guess where I was assigned? Kachin State. Back to the Myitsone again. I just hoped I'd see those rocks in the Malikha River once more.

* * *

During my time in Kachinland, I would be working with the young and running workshops. It reminded me of a seminar I attended in Thailand. Tun must have heard about it somewhere because I'd seen he noted in his diary, 'Ma Thinn will achieve much in her life. That is certain. Us two will surely meet again.'

The day after the youth forum, Mong Ban, Thu Raw and the other girls came to pick me up. The day before, they treated me to Kachin rice and curry at a restaurant, but now we were going to the Myitsone. Along the way, we talked about things that had happened since we'd last met. Each of them had a success story. Some had studied abroad, some had married and were now mothers, others had become wealthy from the famous Kachin jade.

I asked Kaung Mei Mai if she had a boyfriend, but she just smiled and told me nothing extraordinary had happened to her. She in turn asked me how my life had changed over the years, but I decided not to say anything until we got to the Myitsone. They were good girls, they didn't want to upset me by pressing for answers.

The scenery leading up to the Myitsone is indescribably beautiful. Kai Pong Hill had accompanied us all the way from Myitkyina and was still keeping a watchful gaze, unsure whether to let us meet his fiancé the Myitsone without him. And what about the Myitsone herself? Did she doubt us too? Does she believe us our promises to protect her?

We parked the car and walked down the steep bank toward the sand where we ate grilled fish and drank *sapi*. A small motorboat took us out onto the river, up the Ayeyarwaddy to the grey mud triangle that marries the Malikha and Maykha and rises quickly to a promontory crowned with trees. As we beached the motorboat, I saw someone standing on the muddy bank looking right at me. It was Ko Ko Kyaw. I had to control myself; I didn't want to lose face in front of my girls. But how could I avoid this selfish man, on such a narrow strip of land?

"I knew you'd be here today, Thinn," he said, walking up to me.

I said nothing, but screamed silently inside.

"I'd like to talk to you, Thinn."

"I've got nothing to say to you, Ko Ko Kyaw."

"Thinn," he called my name softly.

My girls headed back to the boat so we could talk, but watched closely in case I needed help.

"The rocks are still there in the Myitsone," said Ko Ko Kyaw, pointing to the waters behind me. "The Maykha and the Malikha are still as beautiful as ever."

I knew what he was going to say next.

"May I give my heart to you? I didn't mean to hurt you and – " he paused a moment " – and the one you loved. As time passed, I realise how wrong I was. Could you ever love me in return?" He stood with his back to the Malikha, rocks strewn across the river to the opposite shore behind him. Beneath our feet, grains of sand glittered in the sun. "I come here a lot these days. Whenever I'm here in Myitkyina, whenever I see the beauty of the Myitsone, I remember you, Thinn. I was foolish, jealous of the way you felt towards him, not that I ever stopped loving you."

"Ko Ko Kyaw, let me say one thing," I interrupted, "it's only been three years since Tun died. He's still on my mind. Like you, when I see these rocks in the Malikha, I think of the one who means the most to me. Years ago, when I last was here with you, I was thinking of him. He was still alive then, but even now that he's dead I still keep thinking of him. Tun is still in my heart." Tears spilled over my cheeks.

"Ok, Thinn, I don't want to make you upset. Promise me we'll meet again soon when you've calmed down. Here at the Myitsone, of course."

Ko Ko Kyaw was wrong. Time would never make me love him. I could never love him.

"Sayama... Sayama!" Mong Ban and the others shouted from the motorboat.

"The girls are calling me over," I said, pathetically.

"Thinn, my phone number hasn't changed. Call me if you've got something to say."

I nodded and walked away towards the boat. Soon I was

laughing again with Mong Ban, Thu Raw and the other girls. Kachin Thet Mon Myint started to sing –

"You whom I love most on this earth…
whom I think about and miss you and remember…
So glad we met on the Malikha…"

As the boat pulled away, I looked over at the rocks and saw Tun's face staring back at me. His voice came to me and I listened to his words flow down the Ayeyarwaddy on its thousand-mile journey from Kachinland to the tip of Myanmar. Tun's belief in peace goes with these sacred waters and touches the towns and villages that grow on its banks. A peace Tun never saw, but hopefully I will.

Translated from Burmese by Dr Mirror (Taunggyi)

SAI SAN PYAE

Sai San Pyae (b.1991) is an ethnic Shan writer born in the northern town of Lashio, Shan State. He graduated with a BEng (Mechanical) degree in 2013 from Lashio University of Information and Technology. He currently works as a Basic Computer tutor at the Kham Ku Centre, a Shan youth community organisation housed in the grounds of the Shan Culture and Literature Association.

THUS COME, THUS GONE

The remote hills of northern Shan State are the setting for an uncommon road trip, where four friends encounter ghosts, myths and superstitions in their search for a hidden village. Through simple prose originally written in the Shan Gyi language – and through the journey itself – Sai San Pyae guides his main character Sai Sinn through ever decreasing circles of truth and illusion, change and permanence, leaving the reader in a state of disorientation. It is right that this quest is not lost in the shifting hills but rather reined in, narrowing into a dramatic answer to the question: what happens in the life after this?

THUS COME,
THUS GONE

ပိုင်လူ. ပိုင်လူ.

Gripping a long sword, he surveys his land. Courage etched on his face, clearly he is not one to be intimated. A profound blend of satisfaction, admiration and respect creeps over me whenever that image flashes in mind. He wouldn't have killed his younger brother if not for that band of renegades who made slanderous accusations against the latter. How fascinating his life story would have been!

Oh, our *Saopha*! Is it ignorance that leads us to believe others, exposing ourselves to betrayal and treachery? Time and again throughout Shan history, everything seems so perfect at first. But what comes of it in the end? Nothing but misery. I don't even want to think about the final pages of our history – it only haunts me. According to the *Dhamma*, all things pass: something comes into being only to stop existing; another manifests, then eventually disappears as well – nothing lasts forever. If that's true, I wonder if our broken world will emerge again, fresh and new?

I'm thinking this as I walk, sighing occasionally, lost in contemplation, when something happens. "Ow, you stepped on my foot!"

I turn around to apologise. "Oh, sorry! I didn't mean to, honest." Then with a clear view of her face, my voice suddenly blurts out, "Oh, it's you!"

"You know me?"

She was right to ask the question. How would she know my eyes had followed her on her way to class? "Yes." I still don't know how to answer her question.

"You repair machines in the shop in front of the Shan Literature and Culture Centre, right?" she asks.

"Yes! I mean no. I just go help out my friend with his work," I reply quickly.

"Is that so?" she murmurs.

My friend Sai Pan and I have noticed this girl and her friend for a while now, since they started attending classes near his workplace. I want to get to know her, so I have to think of some words to stop her leaving.

"You come to the festival with friends, don't you, miss?" I said, moving a bit closer to her.

"Yes, of course!" she replied.

Desperately trying to think of some way to prolong the conversation, I look at the nearby booths displaying the rich culture of our people: clay jars, old stone pots, models of long-legged half-timbered houses, then point to one of the booths and say, "Our Shan history is very interesting, don't you think?"

"Definitely!" she says eagerly.

Before she can add anything more, she's interrupted by a shout from across the field, "Mway, come on, we're about to go back home."

"Oh, your name's Mway?" I ask.

"Yes," she replies.

"Mine's Sai Sinn."

"Nice to meet you, Sai Sinn."

"Who's your friend, the one over there?" I point to the girl who shouted and is now walking this way.

"That's Ying Huan."

"Ying Huan," Mway says to her friend, "this is Sai Sinn."

Looking at me, Ying Huan asks, "Did you come to enjoy the festival alone, Sai Sinn?"

"No, I came with my friends."

Sai Nuat and Sai Laet are busy taking photographs of people

at the festival, but Sai Pan is nearby. I call him over and introduce him to the girls.

"Sai Pan? Who repairs machines?" asks Mway.

"Yes, that's me," he answers.

We don't have much time together before she and her friend take their leave to go home. Standing in front of the exhibition room displaying more of our Shan antiques, Sai Pan and I stare at their backs till they disappear from sight.

"Good opportunities never last long," I say to myself.

* * *

"How much do I owe for the photographs, my nephews?"

"Only 500 kyats, auntie."

"Here you are."

"Thanks, auntie. Don't forget your change."

Sai Nuat and Sai Laet seem to be doing well with their business. Camera in hand, Sai Nuat says, "Don't you two want souvenir photos of this Shan New Year? Don't worry, I won't charge you."

Sai Pan replies, "No, we'll pass."

"Fine, if you don't want a photo, then you must want to be beaten. Hey, Sai Laet! Go get a stick to beat them."

Out of nowhere, Sai Laet produces a big stick. Where on earth did he get that? We run away, laughing, "Don't beat us. Ooh, we're so scared…"

* * *

Time passes with never a pause, not even for a second.

During the full moon of the autumn month of *Thadingyut*, those who can warm themselves side by side – no need for the fires lit in worship to the Buddha. I sit alone beside a fire, yet still cannot feel the warmth in my heart. Plus, the rice porridge doesn't taste good.

As the month of *Thabaung* approaches, I don't know whether to sit moping or listen to a distant flute. A light breeze is blowing, but it doesn't make me feel cool. Everything must come and go. I know nothing stays the same forever, I just don't know when things will change.

The full-moon day of the month of the Thabaung is just around the corner, which is probably why the market is so busy. People push their way through the crowds to buy things to donate to the monasteries. Customers at a nearby stall are asking the owner for items they can't find or asking his prices, but he doesn't have time to answer all questions. He also has to keep a detective's eye on everyone, just in case. All generations – children, adolescents and elders – are looking for clothes to wear for the Thabaung Festival. Some merely browse, others stop at various market shops to buy all the necessities for initiating boys into the Buddhist order. During the month of Thabaung, initiation ceremonies can be seen in every town across Shan State, ours included. Adults have only fulfilled their parental duties once their sons have become novices and monks.

Pa Lee calls me over. "Sai Sinn, come help me with my work."

Pa Lee has been my neighbour for a long time.

"What can I do for you, Pa Lee?" I ask.

"Just help Pa Paung load her flatbed tractor. She's a regular customer, and she's bought many gold leaf packets and other things to donate to the pagodas and monasteries."

"Sure thing," I reply.

As the Shan saying goes, 'Shouldering together lightens the load, striving together gets results'. The four of us – Sai Pan, Sai Nuat, Sai Laet and me – help carry everything right behind Pa Paung. After walking a good ways, I speak up: "Pa Paung, you've bought quite a lot of stuff, haven't you?"

"Well, our village is way up in the hills, so I sell these things to villagers who can't go to town so that they will be able to make donations like others."

"For the full moon day of Thabaung?" I continue.

"Yes."

"What's the name of your village, Pa Paung?"

"Wang Lon. It's to the north of here."

"Wang Lon? Then you might know Ying Huan and Ying

Mway. They came here last Shan New Year Festival in the dance group representing Wang Lon."

"Of course, I know them both very well. Ying Mway's my daughter and Ying Huan's one of her best friends. We live quite close to each other."

I don't know whether today is astrologically auspicious or whether it's just plain luck, but I'm very happy to hear the news from Pa Paung. We reach the flatbed tractor that Pa Paung will haul up to Wang Lon.

Pa Paung says, "Thank you all very much for carrying my things."

Before she drives away, I ask her, "Do a lot of visitors go to the Thabaung Festival in your village?"

"Yes, of course."

"Then, if possible, we'd like to visit your village at Thabaung Festival time."

"Do come. I invite all of you."

"But we don't know where you live, Pa Paung."

"Don't worry. Just come to the village monastery, everything will be okay. Even if you don't see me there, I'll ask Aye Huan to pick you up at the monastery.

* * *

The sun gradually struggles out of the valley between the hills. It's a clear warm sunny morning.

Beep, beep! I honk the horn on my bike.

"Sai Laet and Sai Nuat, are you ready? Let's get going!" Sai Pan and I are eager to get to Wang Lon.

"Coming!"

The four of us head out of town on two bikes toward the trail that leads to Wang Lon.

"Sai Sinn, I'm so excited," says Sai Pan. "Ying Huan will be waiting for me. What about you? How's it feel to finally have a chance to see Ying Mway again?"

Sitting behind Sai Pan, I say nothing. I just want to get there as soon as possible. However Sai Nuat and Sai Laet behind us seem relaxed, driving slowly, gazing at the scenery.

Not far along the village trail, we hear traditional Shan drums and cymbals somewhere. It fills us with joy. Scooting up beside us, Sai Nuat honks his horn and says, "Hey, fancy attending the Wang Kan village festival?"

"Been there before," I shout back. "Let's go there on the way home instead."

So we pass by without entering. "Bye bye, Wang Kan."

During the month of Thabaung, farmers burn their fields for the next crop. Smoke rises from the hillsides, filtering sunlight through a haze. Quite a long time after passing Wang Kan, another village appears up ahead.

"Look! We're almost at Pa Paung's village," Sai Laet yells over the noise of the motorcycles.

* * *

The closer we get to the village, the less impressive it seems. At the entrance, an old man stands stiffly staring at us with a curious smile, then holds up his hands in a strange greeting. We don't see a soul around, nothing but dead silence. This can't be Pa Paung's village. The four of us look at each other wondering what's going on. We drive through the village and onto a stony path, all twists and turns. It feels like riding a bucking bull, not a motorcycle. We're tossed this way and that. It's exhausting and we have to be extremely careful, but what did I expect? We're still a developing country. Even the towns and cities have problems, let alone these mountain villages. Has development passed us by and carried on without us?

Sai Nuat and Sai Laet also seem very tired, their faces red with dust. They drive slower and slower. Sai Pan veers off into a dried mud wagon rut.

"Why'd you turn?" I ask him.

"That other path was too bumpy. I thought this one might be better, it might even be a shortcut," he replies and keeps on driving. I make no comment. Looking behind, I see Sai Nuat and Sai Laet following us. After about half an hour, we're glad to see a third small village beckoning in the distance. It's about time. The weather has turned cloudy and gloomy. Suddenly chills run through our bodies: staring right at us is the very same old man we'd seen in the previous village!

We stop our bikes and look at each other in fright. "A ghost is haunting us. It's that same old man we passed, I remember him well. Look! The sky's got even darker." Sai Nuat quickly turns his bike around back down the mud track, but Sai Pan and I are already fleeing in front of them.

"Sai Pan, stop beside that woman carrying a basket."

"I dare not, Sai Sinn. Where did she come from? We didn't see any woman carrying a basket on our way."

"Don't worry. Just stop like I told you."

Sai Pan stops the motorcycle near the woman.

"Could you tell us how to get to Wang Lon, auntie?" I ask.

"You're on the right road. This is the way to Wang Lon."

"Good to know. So where do you live, auntie?"

"In the village you just passed."

Again our skin crawled in fright.

"What's wrong?" she asks. "Why so worried?"

"To be honest, this is our first time up this trail and . . . and, well, it's the second time we've come to this village," I tell her.

"I don't really understand," she says, a puzzled expression on her face.

When I tell her what happened, she looks at us wide-eyed and laughs. "A ghost is haunting you and now you're lost. There's no escape for you now."

"Run!" I shout to the others. "It's another ghost!"

"Don't be silly. Don't run away." The woman shouts back. "Just stop for a moment. I'm no ghost."

We stop our motorcycles again.

"You scared us. You really aren't a ghost, auntie?"

"No, I'm not a ghost. I'm human. You're such cowards. Just show a bit of courage, like real boys. You just took a wrong turn. If you want to get to Wang Lon, keep to the stony path, not this mud one. The old man who smiled at you is just a villager. He's a bit ill, but he's not a ghost."

"Thank you, auntie. We'd better let you go now."

We drove through the village and back onto the stony path.

Bang! We hear a loud noise.

"Was that gunfire?" asks Sai Pan.

"No, it sounded like an explosion."

"An explosion?"

I look behind us. "I think Sai Nuat blew one of his motorcycle tyres. He'll need to fix it."

Fortunately, we brought along repair gear. As we fix the flat, Sai Laet says to Sai Nuat, "I think we're being haunted again."

"Nonsense," I tell him. "There's no ghost. This is just what happens, the truth of impermanence."

Sai Pan gives me a look and tells the others, "Sai Sinn is always talking about this idea of impermanence. What's he usually say? Anything that comes into existence is destined to disappear one day and then something emerges and disappears again."

After replacing the tyre, we continue on our way. Soon, we hear people playing sweet traditional music, drums and cymbals. Paddy fields large and small climb row upon row up the foot of a mountain.

We're relieved to see the words 'Welcome to Wang Lon' written on a plank of wood. After asking some villagers for directions, we drive to the monastery. Everyone who sees us smiles. Are the four of us so handsome? Though once we stop the motorcycles at the monastery to discuss what to do next, we can't help laughing at each other. We're covered head to toe in red dust. So we go and wash at the village bathing pond beside a stream, then go upstairs in the monastery to pay homage to the Buddha image.

We amble down the stairs and go to donate some money. Still no sign of Pa Paung. We ask the man who is minding the silver donation bowl. "Has Pa Paung come to sell gold-leaf packets?"

"You all come from town? Your auntie, Pa Paung, told me you might come visit," he says, then calls out, "Ai Tee, go tell Ying Huan the visitors have arrived. Ask her to pick them up."

Hearing the name Ying Huan, a smile of delight plays over Sai Pan's face.

After looking around the monastery compound, Sai Nuat and

Sai Laet are puzzled why there aren't many people? They come to me and whisper, "Pa Paung said that there'd be a big festival in the village, but we hardly see any people or Pa Paung either."

The donation bowl custodian looks right through us and says, "Hey, Ying Huan *Auon*! Take these boys to see Pa Paung."

We turn around to see Ying Huan. Sai Pan looks, at the same time, astonished and frightened. Sai Nuat and Sai Laet laugh out loud, "Is this the Ying Huan our Sai Pan is always dreaming about? She can't be more than ten or so, ha, ha… !"

What happened? She's not the same Ying Huan. Are we being haunted again? All the people in the compound of the monastery just look at us.

"Hey! What's everybody laughing at?"

We turn round to see who spoke.

"Oh, Pa Paung!"

"You're late," Pa Paung says to us. "Most have already gone to the festival. You'd better follow Lon Pae. Come, come, I'll take you to see him."

"What about our motorcycles, auntie? Can we leave them here?"

"Drive to my house, you can park them inside."

* * *

We jump in the back of a flatbed tractor owned by a Wang Lon villager and ride to a nearby hill. At the top of the hill we reach a crowded pagoda. We hadn't realised the festival would be held on the hill. After paying homage to the pagoda, we go to take a rest in the shade of a big tree.

"You want to find inner peace, don't you? Just look over there," I say to Sai Pan, pointing to a hermit meditating under a tree close to us.

"Yes, you're right," agrees Sai Pan, "Let's go and pay our respects so we may find peace as well."

Afterwards, we ask the hermit, "*Ashin Hpaja,* have you always lived in such a state of peace and tranquillity?"

"*Dajaka,* I'm just trying to find peace, too."

"Ashin Hpaja, you mean even you aren't at peace?"

"True, I'm now enjoying peace, but it only lasts a while. I'm still trying to find eternal peace."

"What does that mean, Ashin Hpaja?" I ask, leaning close to him.

"Everything comes and goes, nothing is permanent. So long as there is birth and death, there can never be an eternal peace. Eternal peace can only be attained through the cessation of the birth and death cycle."

We hear out the rest of his sermon and feel great reverence for him. We ask for permission to take photographs of him.

"Ashin Hpaja, would you please let us take your photograph so we can always pay respects to you, wherever we are?"

"As you wish. Actually, I don't own this body. It will have to be returned to the Lord of Death one day."

The words surprise us, but we all agree, "Yes, one way or another…" Followed by the click-clicking of the camera

* * *

"Hey! Come on. Let's go," Lon Pae calls us over.

By the time we get back onto the flatbed tractor, it's started to rain heavily. The sound of the rain and that of the flatbed tractor merges into a song that accompanies us on our return journey from the pagoda hill.

Sai Pan, Sai Nuat and Sai Laet look at me and say, "So there really is a cycle of birth and death."

"It's not just me always talking about it, you know," I tell them. "Old people talk more, if you just listen. Even when they sneeze or stumble, they always say *Anicca* – Impermanence."

The sound of the rain stops, as does that of the flatbed tractor.

"Get off the flatbed tractor, you young men from the town," says Lon Pae. "We're back at the village."

"Hey, we might live in town, but we're still Shan! Villagers aren't the only true Shan. No matter where we live, we're still Shan, and we won't ever forget we're Shan."

"Come in and have a seat," Pa Paung calls out to us, "No need to hurry back home."

Pa Paung gives us a warm welcome. We're pleased to have Pa Paung as our friend, though we have yet to see Ying Mway or Ying Huan.

"Why were you so late for the festival?" asks Pa Paung as we enter her house.

"We got a flat tyre on the way."

"Ah, that's because only four of you were travelling. Why didn't you get one more to come with you?"

"Why? What's wrong with four people travelling, Pa Paung?" I ask.

"We have a Shan saying, 'Four implies emptiness and nine misses the mark'. Don't you know that?"

"You mean we got a flat tyre because there were just four of us?" asks Sai Pan.

"Definitely! You'd better stay here tonight. There are dark clouds in the sky and I'm worried you'll get drenched on the way. The road will also be too slippery for your motorcycles."

"But we don't want to bother you, Pa Paung."

"Not to worry, we're of the same blood. Make yourselves at home."

We sit out on the balcony of Pa Paung's house, leaning against the bamboo thatched wall and take a rest. I close my eyes and remember the model house I saw at the Shan New Year Festival a year ago. It was exactly like Pa Paung's. Thinking of the Shan New Year Festival reminds me of Ying Mway. "Where are you, Ying Mway?" I ask myself, "I want to see you."

* * *

"You're very late, Ying. Come and help me with the cooking. Huan, come over here, too."

"Coming, mum."

The voice I hear sounds so similar to that of Ying Mway, but I can barely open my eyes, I'm so tired from the journey. I think back to the little girl whom Pa Paung asked to pick us up when we first arrived at the village. She was called Ying Huan, though not the one Sai Pan is fond of. Nor was she the friend of my Ying Mway.

"My elder brothers, my mother asks would you get up and wash yourselves," a voice wakes us the next morning. With great effort, I open my eyes.

"Mway! Is that really Ying Mway? Or am I just dreaming?" I ask out loud.

No, you're not dreaming, a voice inside me answers, *you're wide awake now.*

As if overcome with shyness, Ying Mway goes back into the kitchen. My voice is so loud it wakes my friends with a jolt.

Sai Pan asks me right away, "What did you say, Sai Sinn? Was that Ying Mway?

"Yes," I reply, "it's really her."

"Then Ying Huan will also be…"

"Pa Paung, I'm leaving," Yin Huan's voice suddenly comes from the kitchen. Sai Pan gets up and looks towards the kitchen. Sai Nuat and Sai Laet stare at us two with dazed expressions.

Unfortunately the rain has stopped too early. I wish it would rain forever so the girls can't leave the house. But what can I do? It's the process of emerging and disappearing. Rain emerges and then has to disappear.

After the two girls leave, it's our turn to head home, but my feet are heavy, as if they don't want to lift off the ground. Soon the words etched in wood, 'Farewell from Wang Lon' come into view.

* * *

The full moon day of the month of Thabaung comes and goes without incident. Many other things also come and go, but my thoughts for Ying Mway do not fade away. The moon glows and the stars flicker on high. Where's the Maung Yin Saing Htan Kye constellation? The one that looks like a man shouldering two baskets on a pole, symbolizing the love between Khun San Law and Nang Oo Pyin, two legendary figures whose love for each other can never be broken, even when split apart. "May you two meet again and live happily ever after, Khun San Law and Nang Oo Pyin!" I say to myself.

A few months later, everyone starts putting up their household *chen sam put* – offering shelf. The market is filled with people selling lantern kites, pink and yellow candles, soft and hard fruits. The end of Buddhist Lent is drawing near.

Sai Pan and I are on our motorcycles, smiling. Sai Laet sits quietly behind me and Sai Nuat behind Sai Pan. "Wang Lon!" I yell to the hills, "We're coming to celebrate the end of Buddhist Lent. We bring along Sai Stone this year." Sai Stone isn't a real person, but an actual stone. We give it a name to fool the four-traveller curse.

On arriving in Wang Lon, we sense an eerie silence hanging over the houses. We drive to Pa Paung's house.

"You should've thought twice before you came." Pa Paung says to us. "Aren't you scared?"

"Scared?" we ask, "Why? What's happened?"

"After you left, a dangerous murderer came to the village…" Pa Paung tells us all about him. "The houses at the foot of the pagoda hill have all been deserted. That's why it's so quiet. Ying Mway and Ying Huan are scared, like all the girls around here, they don't dare leave the house. Please, go inside and reassure them that everything will be okay."

"Isn't Lon Pae at home, too?"

"Uncle went with a group of men to catch the murderer, but they've been gone a long time.

* * *

We overhear the next door neighbours talking. "The murderer… They've caught that murderer."

"Where? Let's go have a look. Is he a hideous beast?"

"Good thing they caught him. He can no longer threaten our lives."

The four of us follow the villagers and the buzz of their excited chatter.

"The murderer who destroyed the lives of others will finally see his own life destroyed."

We say to each other, "Everything changes with the passage of time."

Sai Laet says, "Hey, let's take a picture of him, then we can compare him to the hermit we saw last time and see the difference between those who live peacefully and those who live by violence.

"That's a good idea," agrees Sai Pan.

Sai Nuat, however, does not. "A man like him doesn't deserve to be photographed, not with my camera. I just want to beat him with a stick."

We go take a close look at him. He raises his eyes, then lowers them. When we take the picture, he looks up at us again and says, "The four of you have already photographed me twice. Don't you do anything else?" We don't understand until we compare the photographs with the picture of the hermit in our bag.

"Oh, Dear Lord! Exalted Buddha! It's the same man. The criminal is actually the hermit," I exclaim in shock.

Everything changes, nothing is permanent. Transformation itself is the only constant. Whatever exists one day will cease to exist the next.

Translated from Shan Gyi to Burmese by Sai Sang Pe,
and from Burmese to English by Dr Mirror (Taunggyi)

AH PHYU YAUNG (SHWE)

Ah Phyu Yaung (shwe) (b.1973) is the acclaimed author of two short story collections, *Sounds of Knocking (on the door)* (2013) and *The Drowning of a Fairy Horse in Dirty Salty Waters* (2014). She has published 44 stories and essays in wide ranging journals including *Mahaythi, Kalyar, Mahaw Thadar, Pann Alinka, Yanant Thit, Pay Phoo Hlwar and Rati*. In 2006, she was a recipient of the People's Choice Award and in 2016 winner of the prestigious Shwe Amyutae Award for Short Stories.

A FLIGHTPATH FOR SPIRITUAL BIRDS

At the centre of rural life in Myanmar is the village pond; a place to bathe, fish and water animals. It can also be a source of power for the one who controls it. 'A Flightpath for Spiritual Birds' probes and prods this tempestuous relationship between the village and the state, the weak and the powerful. For Ah Phyu Yaung (shwe) religion is no less incorruptible than politics, and the manoeuvrings of the two main characters, the unnamed Abbot and *Saya*, as they strive to heal their community riven by greed and nepotism are paralleled by the tenacious and unbending spirit of the villagers themselves. Her use of the second-person 'you' affects a more personal, intimate encounter, which beautifully descends to a melancholic ending.

A FLIGHT PATH
FOR SPIRITUAL BIRDS

ဝိညာဉ်ငှက်တို့ ပျံသန်းရာ

"Even if they give you money for the pond, you'll still have to buy an engine and petrol. Look at your land. It is flat, so wherever you dig you'll need a pump. Well, let's do it this way. Just tell them to put the pond on my land instead."

"But we'll probably need a large piece of land for it."

"Please don't worry about that. I'll give you as much of my land as you need."

I raised my eyes, spat my *betel* at the base of the roof-post and rinsed my mouth with water. On the table before me was a bubbling glass of Red Bull. I took a sip and looked again at the donor.

I had been at the monastery for little more than year when the foreign reps from the United Nations Development Programme arrived with a project to improve water distribution in the village. They offered to pay for a new pond, but where to put it? The wide green fields out in front of the monastery belonged to the donor, as did the banana groves to the west. The banana trees were up an incline overlooking the monastery, so it would make sense to put a pond there for drainage, but I needed to talk with the donor first.

"My land is higher than yours, by at least eight feet," the donor continued, "so if we put the pond there you won't need a pump or fuel. Just a pipe and the whole monastery compound will receive water."

"Well, yes, but…"

ဝိညာဉ်ဝှက်တို့ ပျံသန်းရာ

"I have plenty of land, so don't feel uneasy. But I do think we should plan things properly from the beginning. We should draw up what to build where, then fence off the site so it's not spoiled. That's what I think anyway."

"Well, do what you think is best."

The donor thought for a minute and said, "The drinking water pond should be close to the street, and the bathing water tank can be, say, 15 feet away. That way, the novices' and monks' bathwater can flow straight to the plants. The pipeline from the drinkable water pond can then be connected to your monastery and people's kitchens. How about this? When the UNDP people come, please just send them to me."

The donor seemed to know what he was doing, so I just nodded. Later, when the foreigners came to the donor's house, he donated a third of his land and the pond was dug as the donor suggested. The monastery received drinking and washing water at no expense.

* * *

It's been nearly a year ago now since that first evening we met, and I have come to know you better, our generous donor. Whenever I walk back to the monastery at dusk, I see what you have written on the back wall of your house.

"Wicked people are more frightening than the Lord of Death himself.

The Lord of Death comes only once, but bad people return again and again."

The road between the monastery and your house leads to the ancient Taung Paw Kyaung pagoda built by King Alaung Sithu. Pilgrims from far away come to pray at the pagoda, so the road is well trafficked. Everyone reads that quote.

Even before I became abbot of this monastery, I was curious about you. After the old abbot died, your name always came up in discussions about who should replace him. It seems the original name of the monastery, Shwe Zedi, faded from memory because of you and your strange vocation, making salt on the high Shan Plateau of all places. By now everyone calls my monastery next to your house the Hsa Hpo Kyaung – 'Saltern Monastery.'

I heard about you from my masters who sent me here to be abbot, as well as from the villagers who came out to greet me when I arrived. Those first few days when I had yet to meet you, I wasn't sure how well you knew the Lord Buddha's *Dhamma*. Some people said you were odd, and being new to the village I was afraid to be seen with you.

During one of my meditation strolls I read and admired your quotes again and I decided to visit you. You sat on a bamboo chair, reading, and said, "Ah, Venerable, you have come to see me, please come in, come in."

I took a seat on one of two benches at your long table and you gave me a glass of water and a glass of Red Bull. Our talk that night was so interesting that I didn't return to the monastery until 8pm. I came to visit you every evening after that. I once asked you about the quote on your wall, but you just said, "Oh, read into it whatever you want. I didn't write it for any special purpose. I read a lot and simply noted down what I like."

I don't know why, but I felt you were hiding the real reason from me.

* * *

One evening, when I arrived at your house, you were writing a letter. Both benches were full of villagers who stood up and paid homage to me before sitting down on the floor.

"We were asking *Saya* for advice about the road, O Venerable One," they explained. "The abbot of the eastern monastery has blocked the street, so no person or animal can get through east of the creek. We tried to negotiate with the abbot but he won't listen. This road is a shortcut from our homes to the fields. If we can't go this way, we'll have to cross the creek to the south, but that means walking through others' plots, which is asking for trouble in the rainy season. O Venerable One, we are not educated men. All we know is the soil and cows and which crops to grow in which season. That's why we came to *Saya* for help, even though it's not his problem. His land is at this end of the road, not the other end like ours."

"But why did the abbot block the road?" I asked.

You pointed to the big trees along the far side of your compound and the forested hill behind. I saw a new pagoda being built in the style of the Mahabodhi Pagoda at Bodhgaya.

"Venerable One," you began, "as you can see, my compound is big. The road the villagers are talking about passes between my compound and the eastern monastery. The road is actually an oxcart track that ends at the creek, then turns into a walking path from there into the village. Everyone from the eastern side of the village who come to your monastery or go to the Taung Paw Kyaung Pagoda on the other side of my compound take this route. It's been this way for a long time. Now that the abbot from the eastern monastery has blocked the street, pilgrims have to make a long detour. It's possible on foot, but not with carts and cows. So although my farm lands are not affected, this is why I want to help."

"Okay, how far along are you?"

"Well, we don't know how powerful this abbot is, but we do know the commander-in-chief is his disciple. The ruling party isn't listening either, so now I am drafting a letter to the State Monks' Association."

According to the villagers, the eastern monastery had once been very small, just a simple building on the slope. Then, little by little, the monastery grew until it devoured the whole hill.

In the teachings of the Lord Buddha it is written that all one needs is a single tree or cave. I didn't want to disturb you or the villagers with pedantry, so I returned to the monastery without our evening talk.

* * *

The next day I saw you leaving with your little bag. In the evening I awaited your return from town, looking over the monastery wall to your compound planted with so many vegetables and fruit trees. Flowers grew wild around your house, and like the flowers blooming in many colours, so too the villagers wrestled with their many different thoughts at your house. I couldn't wait alone anymore and so I joined them, thinking to myself, "If the village has a problem, then I also have a problem – even if I am a monk."

Tin Win from the third house over saw me coming and invited me in. "O Venerable One, please have some tea! *Saya*'s not back yet. We're all waiting for him."

"Yes, I know, that's why I'm here. I must admit, he is very persistent."

"Oh yes, you know, the same thing happened to him once. He used to own about four acres of land along the Shwe Nyaung-Taunggyi Road. He never got it back. He complained right up to the central authorities, but he still lost. He's tough. He has a seasonal fruits and timber plantation, an oil mill, a saw mill and a saltern. We all envy him a little, but we can't work hard like him, so we 'eat without salt'. Whenever we have problems we always come to him first, we drink his tea and discuss whatever is bothering us."

While we were talking, you suddenly came in with your little bag. It was dark outside, as was the expression on your face. We all knew what had happened, though none of us had the courage to ask. We all went quiet.

"Venerable One, have you been here long? I couldn't get a bus back, so I had to hitchhike part way on a lime truck and walk the rest, that's why I'm so late." You then turned to the waiting villagers and simply said, "When you are the anvil, you must endure the hammer. Am I right?"

I could not bear to see the hopeless faces of the villagers, so I walked back slowly to the monastery.

* * *

"Wicked people are more frightening than the Lord of Death himself.

The Lord of Death comes only once, but bad people return again and again."

I no longer need to ask why you wrote that.

Translated from Burmese by Khin Hnit Thit Oo

GLOSSARY

Abhidhammā the philosophy of the Buddha's teachings, the last of three canons in Buddhist scripture (Pali)

Ashin Hpaya a term used to address or refer to the Buddha or a monk (Burmese)

auon 'little' or 'younger' (Shan)

betel areca nuts, lime and tobacco wrapped in a betel leaf and chewed as a mild stimulant (Burmese)

Bo 'Lieutenant' (Burmese)

chen sam put small, raised altar for religious offering (Burmese)

cheroot untapered hand-rolled cigar of varying sizes (Burmese)

chinlon a cane ball (Burmese)

Dajaka a term used by a monk to address an ordinary person (Burmese)

de rhe ban ne 'hello' (Kayah)

Dhamma the holy teachings of the Lord Buddha (Pali)

Don Yein a dance involving multiple participants performed on New Year's Day and other important occasions (Karen)

Duwa a hereditary clan chief (Jinghpaw)

hmaw 'mine' (Jinghpaw)

hongsa mythical Indian aquatic bird; national symbol of the Mon people (Mon)

hpa see Karen bronze drums decorated with images of frogs (Burmese)

htamein a long piece of cotton cloth wrapped around the waist for women (Burmese)

Jinghpaw the most numerous of the six ethnic nationality groups who make up the Kachin people (Jinghpaw)

Kahprek a form of martial arts practised by the Kachin people (Jinghpaw)

Kamma Known mostly as Karma (Sanskrit) in English, the principle by which the actions of an individual effects the future of that individual (Pali)

Kason the second month of the Myanmar lunar calendar year in honour of the Buddha attaining enlightenment (Burmese)

law pan a wealthy man (Jinghpaw)

loca refers to the 'world' or the human realm (Pali)

lone 'uncle'; respectful honorific for an older man (Shan) *longyi* a long piece of cotton cloth wrapped around the waist (Burmese)

Manau Kachin New Year festival held in January (Jinghpaw)

maww 'mother' (Kayah)

mingalaba 'hello' (Burmese)

pa 'aunt'; respectful honorific for an older woman (Shan)

pandals temporary wooden stages built during New Year celebrations (Burmese)

Patthāna Buddhist texts on causal relationships (Pali)

sai common honorific for young men (Shan)

Sangha the state monastic community of monks or nuns (Pali)

Saopha 'chief' or 'ruler' (Shan)

sapi wine made from fermented rice (Jinghpaw)

Sasana a term used by Buddhists when referring to their religion (Pali)

Saya a male teacher or respected older man (Burmese)

Sayadaw a teacher ordained as a Buddhist monk (Burmese)

Sayama a female teacher or respected older woman (Burmese)

sra male teacher/respected older man (Jinghpaw)

Thabaung twelfth and last month of Myanmar lunar calendar year (Burmese)

Thadingyut the seventh month of the Myanmar lunar calendar celebrating the descent of Buddha to the human realm (Burmese)

thanakha popular cream-coloured paste made from tree bark and applied on the face and arms as a sunscreen (Burmese)

Thasaungmon the month after the Buddhist Lent (Burmese)

Thingyan water-throwing festival preceding Burmese New Year (Burmese)

ye-ma-sei unwashed stones (Burmese)

ying 'girl' (Shan)

TRANSLATOR AND EDITOR BIOGRAPHIES

AUNG MIN KHANT

Aung Min Khant (b.1996) was born in Yangon. A final-year student majoring in English at the Yangon University of Foreign Languages, he is a graduate of the 2015 Link the Wor(l)ds literary translation programme. Though only 21 years old, his Burmese-to-English translations include six essays from *November 8th Diary* (NDSP, 2016) a literary exploration of the historic national elections.

DR MIRROR (TAUNGGYI)

Dr Mirror (Taunggyi) (b.1978) is a medical doctor, writer and translator from Shan State. He is a graduate of the 2015 Link the Wor(l)ds literary translation programme and has collaborated with PEN Myanmar on the well-received 2016 book, *November 8th Diary*, translating three works on the historic national elections.

KHIN HNIT THIT OO

Khin Hnit Thit Oo (b.1979) is a translator, tour guide and social entrepreneur. She is a graduate of the 2015 Link the Wor(l)ds literary translation programme. She was recently invited to France to collaborate on a two-month-long memoir-translation project. She is currently writing a bilingual non-fiction novel about Burmese society.

LETYAR TUN

Letyar Tun (b.1972) is a writer, translator, photojournalist and former political prisoner. He spent 18 years in prison (14 years on death row) for his political activism. Since his release in 2012, his stories have appeared in multiple journals, his photography has been exhibited in Myanmar and he has spoken on freedom of expression at events across South East Asia. He is a graduate of the 2015 Link the Wor(l)ds literary translation programme and recently gained a scholarship to study at the inaugural School for Interpretation and Translation in Yangon. He currently works for Fojor Media Institute in Yangon.

SAN LIN TUN

San Lin Tun (b.1974) is a writer born in Yangon from Mon-Burmese parents. A graduate of the 2015 Link the Wor(l)ds literary translation programme, his fiction has appeared in numerous local and international publications including the New Asian Writing Anthology. He is the author of ten books in English, including the short novel *Walking Down an Old Literary Road* (Mudita Books, 2008) and the short-story collection *A Classic Night at Café Blues and Other Stories* (Mudita Books, 2010). His latest book, a collection of essays entitled *Reading a George Orwell Novel in a Myanmar Teashop* was published in 2016.

U YE HTUT

(b.1949) is an award winning dramatist, translator and academic. Professor Emeritus of Dramatic Literature at the National University of Arts and Culture, Yangon, his most recent work is the bilingual 'A comparative study of Sale U Ponnya's Water-Seller and Shakespeare's The Merchant of Venice'.

LUCAS STEWART

Lucas Stewart is a former British Council literature adviser, working in Myanmar from 2011 to 2016 with writers, publishers and booksellers during the transition. He is the author of *The People Elsewhere: Unbound Journeys with the Storytellers of Myanmar* (Penguin/Viking, 2016) and has written on ethnic language literature for several international publications. A Fellow of the Royal Asiatic Society he recently left Asia after more than 15 years and now lives in Khartoum. He writes at www.sadaik.com

ALFRED BIRNBAUM

Alfred Birnbaum studied Burmese at SOAS and the Institute of Foreign Languages, Yangon. He lived in Myanmar for six years from 1995 while promoting Burmese lacquerware for the Japanese market, organising the first show of Myanmar contemporary painting in Japan, and initiating efforts to document early modern architecture in Yangon. Together with his wife Thi Thi Aye, he translated the contemporary Burmese novel *Smile as They Bow* by Nu Nu Yi Inwa, shortlisted for the 2007 Man Asian Literary Prize. Recently, under the combined auspices of PEN Myanmar, the British Centre for Literary Translation, Writers' Centre Norwich and the British Council, he led short-story translation workshops, which helped to foster some of the talents in this collection. He currently lives in Tokyo, where he works as a literary translator and writer.

ACKNOWLEDGEMENTS

The genesis of the *Hidden Words, Hidden Worlds* project from which these stories sprang was in 2012 and it has only reached its conclusion five years later with this publication of the English edition. Over these years, many individuals and organisations, from Yangon, from the ethnic states and from outside Myanmar have contributed, guided and advised.

A definitive reckoning of all the hands that have touched these stories in some way would run to a length greater than the stories themselves; but the British Council would like to thank in particular those below who, without whom, this English edition would not have been possible:

In Yangon: Daw Zin Mar Oo, the Kantkaw Education Centre and their students Nyan Lawi, N Zaw Jum, Van Bawi Thawng, Mu Caroline, Tha Iang Len, Tin Han Kyaw and in particular Nhkum Bawk Nu Awng and Tha Htoo Myat; Myo Min Tun@Last Leaf Gallery, Dr Ma Thida (Sanchaung) and the members of PEN Myanmar, Dr Thant Thaw Kaung from Myanmar Book Centre, Professor Khin Maung Cho, Saw Hser Ka Taw, Htu Seng Aung, Agoon Soil Thipa.

Beyond Yangon: Naw F Tana Paw, Ko Zayar Aung and all the Hpa-an Millennium Centre volunteers; Saw Chit Than, Mahn Lin Myat Kyaw and the Karen Culture and Literature Association; Ko Min Latt, Kyi Zaw Lwin and all the Mawlamyine Centre volunteers; Mie Lay Mon, Ajar Min Aung Zay, Min Min Nwe, Nai Maung Toe and the Mon Literature and Culture Committee; S Khon Mai and all the Myitkyina Millennium Centre volunteers; Rev. N-Gan Tang Gun, Duwa Walu Sin Wa and all the members of the Kachin Culture and Literature Co-operation Committee, the Kachin Baptist Convention, Kachin Dictionary Committee and the Wunpawng Shingni; U Myo Aung, Nang Khey Sett and all the Lashio Millennium Centre volunteers; Sai Hseng Mong, Daw Nang Voe Seng, Sai Sang Pe and the Shan Literature and Culture Association; Cung Mang and all the Hakha Millennium Centre volunteers; Rev. Taan Mang and the Chin Association for Christian Communication; Nyi Nyi Naing, Ko Wi Zin Yo and all the Loikaw Millennium Centre volunteers; Poe Reh, Cember Paw@Maw Ko Myar and Plu Reh from the Kayah National Literacy and Culture Committee; R G Nyi Nyi Tun and his volunteers at the Youth Life Formation Centre; Kyan Zin Myay Saw Khet, Pho Kyawt, Daw Saw Khin Tint and Dr San Hla Kyaw from Rakhine Culture and Literature Association.

Beyond Myanmar: PEN International, Writers' Centre Norwich, Asia Literary Review, Asia House, Jon Wilcox and James Byrne.

We would also like to thank the Arts team and others at the British Council for their support and collaboration over the years: Daw Kyi Kyi Pyone, Ne Chye Thwin, Thin Aung Htoo, Daw Moe Moe Soe, Kevin McKenzie, Susana Galvan and Rebecca Hart.

Finally, a special note of remembrance must be made for those writers who passed away before the publication of this English edition: Pao Lao, Dr Khin Pann Hnin and Saw Lambert.